BACCANO!

1931 Winter: The Time of Oasis

RYOHGO NARITA

ILLUSTRATION BY
KATSUMI ENAMI

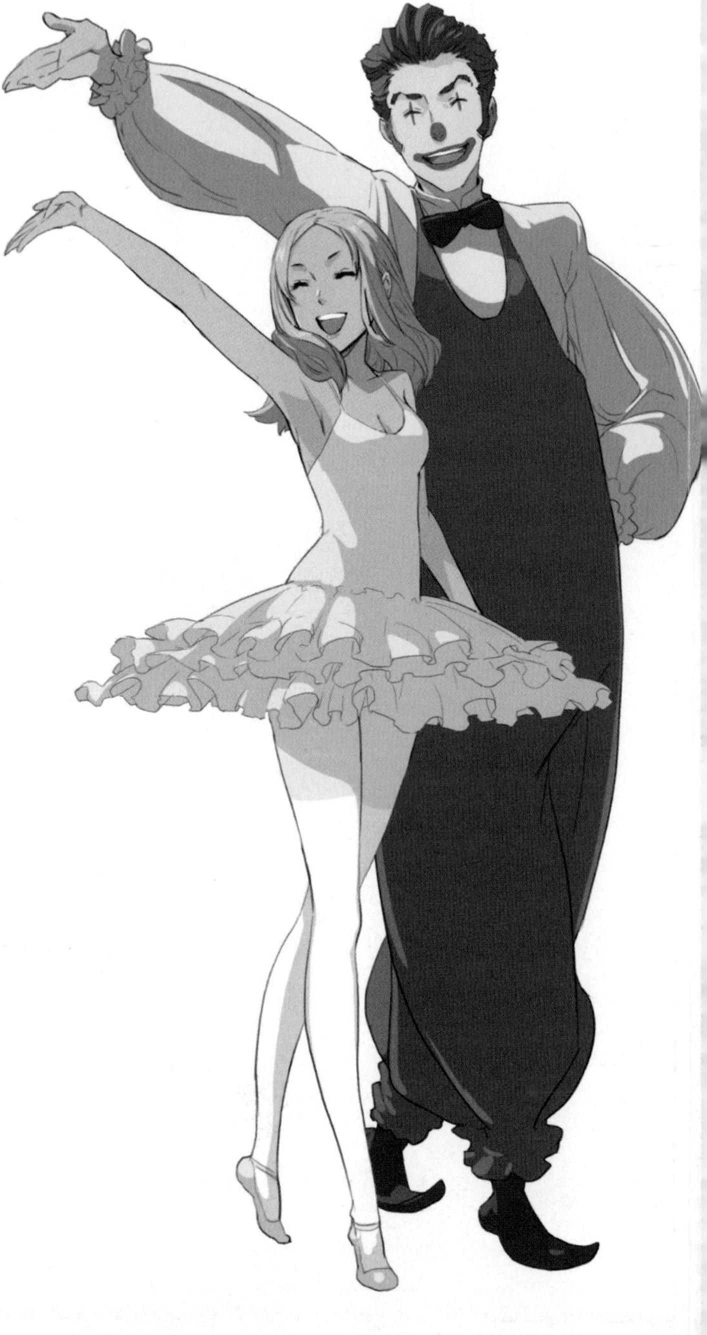

BACCANO!

1931 Winter: The Time of the Oasis

VOLUME 20

RYOHGO NARITA
ILLUSTRATION BY **KATSUMI ENAMI**

YEN ON

NEW YORK

BACCANO!, Volume 20: 1931 Winter: THE TIME OF THE OASIS
RYOHGO NARITA

Translation by Taylor Engel
Cover art by Katsumi Enami

This book is a work of fiction. Names, characters, places, and incidents
are the product of the author's imagination or are used fictitiously. Any
resemblance to actual events, locales, or persons, living or dead, is coincidental.

BACCANO! Vol.20
©Ryohgo Narita 2013
Edited by Dengeki Bunko
First published in Japan in 2013 by KADOKAWA CORPORATION, Tokyo.
English translation rights arranged with KADOKAWA CORPORATION, Tokyo,
through Tuttle-Mori Agency, Inc., Tokyo.

English translation © 2022 by Yen Press, LLC

Yen On
150 West 30th Street, 19th Floor
New York, NY 10001

Visit us at yenpress.com
facebook.com/yenpress
twitter.com/yenpress
yenpress.tumblr.com
instagram.com/yenpress

First Yen On Edition: October 2022
Edited by Carly Smith & Yen On Editorial: Anna Powers
Designed by Yen Press Design: Wendy Chan

Yen On is an imprint of Yen Press, LLC.
The Yen On name and logo are trademarks of Yen Press, LLC.

The publisher is not responsible for websites (or their content) that are not owned by the publisher.

Library of Congress Cataloging-in-Publication Data
Names: Narita, Ryōgo, 1980– author. | Engel, Taylor, translator.
Title: Baccano! / Ryohgo Narita ; translation by Taylor Engel.
Description: First Yen On edition. | New York : Yen On, 2016–
Identifiers: LCCN 2015045300 | ISBN 9780316270366 (v. 1 : hardback) |
ISBN 9780316270397 (v. 2 : hardback) | ISBN 9780316270410 (v. 3 : hardback) |
ISBN 9780316270434 (v. 4 : hardback) | ISBN 9780316558662 (v. 5 : hardback) |
ISBN 9780316442275 (v. 6 : hardback) | ISBN 9780316442312 (v. 7 : hardback) |
ISBN 9780316442329 (v. 8 : hardback) | ISBN 9780316442343 (v. 9 : hardback) |
ISBN 9780316442367 (v. 10 : hardback) | ISBN 9781975356859 (v. 11 : hardback) |
ISBN 9781975384715 (v. 12 : hardback) | ISBN 9781975384739 (v. 13 : hardback) |
ISBN 9781975384753 (v. 14 : hardback) | ISBN 9781975384777 (v. 15 : hardback) |
ISBN 9781975321567 (v. 16 : hardback) | ISBN 9781975321901 (v. 17 : hardback) |
ISBN 9781975321925 (v. 18 : hardback) | ISBN 9781975321949 (v. 19 : hardback) |
ISBN 9781975321963 (v. 20 : hardback)
Subjects: CYAC: Science fiction. | Nineteen twenties—Fiction. | Organized crime—Fiction. |
Prohibition—Fiction. | BISAC: FICTION / Science Fiction / Adventure.
Classification: LCC PZ7.1.N37 Bac 2016 | DDC [Fic]—dc23
LC record available at http://lccn.loc.gov/2015045300

ISBNs: 978-1-9753-2196-3 (hardcover)
978-1-9753-2197-0 (ebook)

1 2022

LSC-C

Printed in the United States of America

Come, let's begin the hunt.

Swing your blade; drive your prey before you.
Run twisterly, wavagly, loppely.
Don't overtake it, even when it's in your grasp.
Don't let it escape, even when it's slipping away.
Run swiftig, stumblect, dronkily.
When the rabbit is tired, raise your blade.
The little rabbit is spent.
The strength is yours. The kill is yours.
What you need are courage and hope.
Kill that exhausted rabbit.
First kill the rabbit, next kill a pig.
Take the pig's head, then take a deer's.
Until a man or a monster awaits you.
Large or small, array yourselves before us, blessings of the land.
Cut them apart bravely.
Be greedy, be grateful.

Come, let's begin the hunt.

Digression

1924   A rural district on the outskirts of Chicago

"Hey, Nader! Put away those tools! Rain's coming!"

"I know, Pa. Just hold on a second," the boy answered.

Nader, who was in his early teens, headed for the shed with an armful of farm tools. Halfway there, he paused. "Oh…"

There was a house a short distance away, and he'd seen a girl leaving with her mother. The girl looked a few years younger than him, and she wore an amiable smile. Her mother drew her by the hand as they walked toward the woods. The girl carried a long, thin cloth sack over her shoulder. It looked pretty heavy, and it was almost as long as she was tall. She staggered a little under it, as if the bag were carrying her instead, but still she wore that innocent expression.

Once she spotted Nader, the girl waved at him vigorously. "Ahhh! It's Naaader! G'mooorning."

Nader vaguely raised a hand in response, but she didn't go over to him. She got farther away, pulled along by her mother.

"Oh…" The boy lowered his hand a bit sadly.

He watched his childhood friend until she became small in the distance. Then his father smacked him on the back, and he came to himself with a jolt.

"Waugh!"

"What're you woolgathering for, boy?"

"S-sorry, Pa."

The boy hastily resettled the tools in his arms and started for the shed again. "Say, Pa? Sonia's been going out with her ma a lot these days. Where do you s'pose they go?"

His father didn't answer. He just walked along silently. Puzzled, Nader followed. Finally, when they were near the shed, the man broke his silence. "...Maybe you shouldn't have too much to do with them."

"Why?"

"Poor Sonia... Her folks seem really, uh... Well, you know. They weren't so bad before, but... Lately, they've been sorta... Hmm." His father hemmed and hawed.

That didn't satisfy Nader, but as he tried to press him for details, something cold struck his arm.

"Whoa, here it comes."

He and his father both ran for the shed.

Nader figured it wasn't a big deal, so he didn't ask about the girl's parents again.

It would be a while before the boy found out what his childhood friend's life had been like.

⟺

An hour later

Deep in the woods, a dull gunshot rang out through the steady rain.

The long-barreled gun looked out of place in the girl's mud-smeared hands. Not only was it a deadly weapon, but it seemed too big for a child to be firing at all.

She must have been shooting for quite a while: The raindrops that struck the end of the barrel evaporated, generating a thin haze reminiscent of gun smoke.

"What do you think, Sonia? Doesn't shooting in the rain feel completely different?" her mother asked.

The girl seemed to be done for now; she'd taken out her earplugs. She puffed out her cheeks, dissatisfied. "Ugh... I can't hit it at aaaall."

"That's okay, Sonia. I can't teach you any tricks, and you can shoot however you want. Hit your mark or don't; anything's fine."

The girl was still on her stomach in the mud. Her mother knelt beside her and stroked her small head, smiling gently.

"You're free. You don't even have to go to school.

"You just keep on shooting, as much as you want."

⟺

Night   The girl's house

The girl's father patted her head, just as her mother had done. "Oh, you have that nice smell on you, Sonia. Like a smoking gun."

She smiled happily. The man was lying in bed, and she hugged his arm tight.

A daughter sharing a moment with her dad as he drifted off to sleep. In a way, the scene might have looked heartwarming…if it hadn't been for all the bandages on the man's body and the countless bullet scars peeking between the gaps.

Even then, someone could believe the scene was a daughter visiting her injured father—except dozens of rifles and handguns on the walls surrounding the bed struck that possibility off the list as well.

The master of this gun-filled room gently stroked his daughter's cheek. It would be easy to assume he was a kind father. "Sonia, do you like firing guns?"

"Uh-huh! 'Cause you and Mommy are so proud of me when I do it!"

"Indeed we are. You're a good girl, Sonia." The man turned affectionate eyes on his beloved daughter. "Listen, Sonia. You don't have to go to school, all right? Making friends, finding romance—that stuff can wait, too."

Speaking with love, he planted a peculiar "belief" in his daughter's heart.

"Treasure these guns. You'll never have to worry as long as you've got one to fire. If anyone tries to shoot you, you can shoot 'em right back. If times get tough, you can even go on the kill yourself. Don't believe in addition or subtraction, history or science, the gospel or the law, Daddy or Mommy. Believe in guns, Sonia. That's all you need to live a happy life."

"Huh? I don't really get it," the young girl told him honestly.

Her father stroked her head again, and his voice as he spoke to her was very warm for the topic. "It's okay if you don't understand. As long as you have a gun, there's no need to worry. Your daddy and mommy are happy because we have guns, too.

"You see, Sonia...guns are our god."

⇔

Nader had no idea.

He knew nothing about the curse that had been placed on his childhood friend—a girl who didn't even go to school—while she was growing up. He made tracks out of that village and left the girl behind, and it would be quite a while before he heard about her history.

In 1935, during a certain incident in New York, the grown-up girl and boy would meet again.

They'd come very close to meeting before then, though. Just once.

This is the story of an event the girl was pulled into.

It had put her very near the boy, with the train known as the Flying Pussyfoot between them—an incident that set the girl on her course into fate's enormous vortex.

But the girl wasn't dragged in all by herself.

PROLOGUES

Prologue 1   **The Rabbit Hutch**

1931   The outskirts of Newark

The local kids thought of him as a prince in the mansion deep in the forest…

It was both a compliment and stinging sarcasm. The boy was the direct descendant of someone powerful, and in another world, he actually would have been called a prince.

However, this "someone powerful" was the type who never left the shadows.

Only one thing inconvenienced the boy: the rule that restricted his world.

Whatever he wanted, he could have.

His grandfather was a firm believer in good manners, and he could be strict. On the other hand, the boy's parents were soft on him; they'd buy him anything he asked for, provided it was something ordinary people could acquire.

And yet the boy was never satisfied.

He could have been content with this close-range "freedom" and become outrageously spoiled—yet he had just one selfish wish. This desire occupied his thoughts to such a degree that he had none to spare for being spoiled.

*   *   *

He wanted to venture outside the walls by himself.

He didn't mind if it was only for a few hundred yards.

He wanted to wander freely around outside the house on his own. That was all he asked for, but he was not allowed. Despite his pleas, the boy was always a bird in a cage.

He wasn't a prisoner. His parents loved him quite well enough, and that was why he wasn't allowed to be alone. He was surrounded by a throng of people, but his desire for solitude left him lonely.

No one noticed his growing melancholy, not even him.

His parents were well aware that the matter was probably weighing on his mind, and yet they never left him alone.

…Why?

Fundamentally, it was because he was the direct descendant of someone powerful.

Carzelio Runorata, nicknamed Cazze.

The name the boy had been given also determined his status.

The Runorata Family was a mafia syndicate based out of Newark. Led by Bartolo Runorata, the enormous organization had well over a thousand members. That authority was very real, but it was never exercised in the full light of day.

The name "Runorata" marked its bearers as part of that authority.

When future generations looked back on this time, many of them would call it the era of Prohibition.

People had wanted that particular law for various reasons. Some groups considered alcohol a vice, while others wanted a check on Germany, a nation of brewers. Noble ideals and shrewd politics tangled together in complicated ways, and for a brief moment in history, the country became a "dry society."

However, the results were deeper social vice and a giant power that began to feed on it and gain strength.

Up until then, alcohol had been a common indulgence, but the shackles of the Prohibition Act turned it into a treasure. Alcohol became as valuable as jewels. The phrase *fine, forbidden drink* took on a literal sense.

Even those who'd never tasted liquor before were caught up in this guilty pleasure amid the enormous social current, and they began crowding into speakeasies along with the lushes.

Ironically, although part of the law's intent had been to reduce crimes committed by drunks, it ended up criminalizing once-innocent citizens.

On top of that, the Great Depression had struck America a harsh blow, and the constant anxiety turned more and more people to alcohol.

That said, while the lights of the speakeasies shone, "heroes" with the power to repel the Great Depression were growing in their shadows. The general public tended to lump them together as "the mafia." These gangsters didn't just slip through the law's net; they openly tore right through it, amassing great power through the sale of bootleg liquor.

Essentially, the government's Prohibition Act became a convenient hotbed that helped these enemies of the law make rapid social advances.

They used their power violently, chivalrously, eloquently.

Fostered by the chains of Prohibition, these forces strode through the underbelly of society.

The "family" into which the boy had been born—the Runorata Family—held part of this power.

The enormous organization had expanded its influence across the American East in the blink of an eye, putting down roots with the help of the Prohibition Act. The boy had only just turned nine, but even he vaguely understood that he belonged to the peculiar world known as the mafia.

Still, Cazze couldn't have cared less.

He wasn't sent to school. Instead, he had knowledge drummed into him by private tutors.

…And yet, whenever a large party was held at his house, all the locals attended, and it became the sort of gala that was discussed in books and on the radio.

Cazze met other children there, but they only greeted him because their parents told them to, and they treated him as something fundamentally different from themselves.

As a matter of fact, as far as the local kids were concerned, Cazze was a prince. He didn't go to school, but it wasn't because he was poor. When they talked to him, he spoke more clearly than they did, and he knew twice as much. In the children's minds, if he wasn't a "prince," nobody was.

Ordinarily, they were told they mustn't go near the Runorata Family's enormous mansion.

At the parties, their own parents all paid their respects to its residents.

A castle in the forest. A child more refined than anyone they'd ever seen at school.

He was like a character from a fairy tale. Some kids called him a prince out of jealousy, and others did it because they idolized him.

Either way, though, they never saw the boy before the next party, and if they tried to go to him, their parents stopped them in no uncertain terms. Gradually, they even forgot what the so-called prince looked like.

After several years of this, the craving in Cazze's heart was growing stronger by the day.

Thanks to his private education, he knew a little more than other children his age, and he was a bit more mature—but he wasn't yet ten years old. He was too young to put his discontent into eloquent words. All he knew was that he wanted to go outside.

The magnificent mansion had a fountain in its expansive gardens, and all sorts of people lived there with Cazze and his family. Bartolo Runorata, his grandfather, lived with them, and so did his children and their families—but there was no one Cazze's age.

His mother was Bartolo's oldest daughter, and Cazze's cousins were still too young to really talk to. He took care of them and played with them, but they were nothing like the sort of friends he wanted.

Besides, not even having a friend around would have changed the fact that he couldn't go outside.

When he went for a walk, someone always went along to guard him.

If he looked around, he could see multiple guards around him, all at a distance. This made walks rather uncomfortable, and the claustrophobic sense of being watched every waking moment squeezed his young mind like a vise.

And then—he snapped.

⇔

December 30, 1931   Noon   Somewhere in New Jersey

"Ghk...ah... *Hff*..."

A small figure ran, panting for breath.

Cazze's fine clothes were already a little grubby here and there. He dove into the bushes and clapped his hands over his mouth, forcing himself to breathe quietly.

"Was he there?"   "No."   "He's not over here, either."
    "Where did he go?!"   "Don't tell me the Gandors—"
"No, it sounds like he left by himself."   "What for?!"
    "That's nuts!"   "First things first: We need to report this to the boss..."

The distant clamor gradually came closer, passed right by the boy's hiding place, and was gone.

About ten minutes earlier, Cazze had dangled over the window a rope ladder he'd secretly constructed, escaping in broad daylight.

Carefully, he made his way through the bushes, moving slowly as he held his breath. The voices came back. He stiffened again.

*   *   *

"Goddammit."   "Send out the cars."

    "Get the word out."   "Hold it."

"We can't afford to let this commotion spread."

"It's too fuckin' late for that! The situation's already ugly, both for the boy and for us!"

     "Nothing from the boss yet?"   "Hurry! We have to find him, no matter what."

"Even if he did run away, whatever you do, don't let any other outfits hear about it…"

The voices were searching for him desperately. Cazze felt guilty, but his resolve was unshaken.

Out.

I'm getting out.

Scanning his surroundings carefully, he crept through the bushes, gradually putting distance between himself and the mansion.

Ba-dump—

His heart leaped.

I'm free, free, free!

He screamed the word in his mind, over and over.

No matter how grand it was, a mansion he couldn't leave might as well have been a rabbit hutch.

Just once would be enough, the boy prayed.

It was the world's most luxurious rabbit hutch. He might starve and die outside it, but he didn't think about that. He didn't have the time or the spare energy to think.

He'd taken walks down this path many times before, and he was delighted by how different both it and the surroundings looked now.

That said, he'd barely registered the landscape those other times. He'd been focused on the people around him, so of course the view seemed new. Cazze was still a kid, though, and he didn't have it in him to think that far. He just let the novelty of the experience intoxicate him.

The boy turned to check behind him, made sure none of the mansion's men were in sight—

—and then took off down a deer track through the woods, running as hard as he could.

Run, run, run.

Runrunrunrunrunrun, he yelled to himself silently.

He wasn't thinking about what might come next.

If a truck passes, I'll hide in the back and go far away. The boy only had a vague plan as he kept on running through the forest.

He wasn't thinking about whether he'd be able to come back.

He was still focused on what lay ahead.

Believing that something magnificent was waiting for him on the bright road beyond the trees, the boy ran and ran and ran.

And when he emerged from the woods, he found something perfect: A small truck with a canvas back was stopped on the side of the road.

The boy glanced over his shoulder, making sure that the mansion's people still hadn't spotted him.

With a whispered "Sorry," he climbed into the bed of the truck.

When it came down to it, the boy genuinely didn't understand the position he held.

He didn't know what sort of value the world would place on him—or how much danger he would be in as a result.

Given that he was Bartolo Runorata's grandson, it wasn't a stretch to assume that Cazze would be responsible for that enormous family in a few decades. As a matter of fact, he was the strongest candidate in his generation.

Even disregarding that, Bartolo's relatives would be extremely enticing *bargaining chips* to his enemies.

Oblivious to the fact that his head was worth so much…

…filled with hope, the boy fled the too-large rabbit hutch imprisoning him—and escaped into the outside world.

Prologue 2　　　　Vanishing Bunny

Meanwhile　　On the outskirts of Newark

"So is that really going to work?"

"Oh, it'll be fine! The word *failure* isn't in my dictionary!"

"Maybe that's why you never learn anything from it."

"Wha—? Just a— Listen, you!"

"Quit fiiighting."

Rattle, clank. Rattle, clank. Rattle, clank. Ka-tunk.

A truck with a canvas back and a rattletrap engine bounced noisily down the country road.

It was traveling through the forests of Newark on purpose, taking roads that could just barely accommodate a single vehicle. Inside it, three women were having a loud and lively conversation. Two of them sat in the cab, while the third was poking her head in from the bed of the truck.

The woman in the driver's seat had a ponytail and was about twenty years old. "So, Lana," she asked the woman in the passenger seat, yawning, "is it really going to work?"

It was the same question she'd asked a minute ago, and the other woman's temples twitched. "Huh? Excuse me? Why did you repeat yourself? Huh? Why did you ask that again?!"

Lana appeared to be in her early twenties, and she wore glasses. Her sharp eyes made her look older, which meant her actual age might have been the same as the driver's.

"'Why' isn't the question. I'm just trying to add the word *failure* to that bum dictionary of yours."

"Excuse you?! What's that supposed to mean, Pamela?! Define *bum*!!"

"Wow, it doesn't even have *bum* in it… I swear. Aren't people who wear glasses supposed to be smart? It's total fraud." Pamela, the woman with the ponytail, gave a disgusted sigh and shot a pitying glance at Lana.

Meanwhile, Lana was getting more and more worked up. She clenched her fists. "That is not what I meant when I said that!" she howled. "Also, excuse me?! You discriminate because of people's glasses?! That's…spectaclist!"

"Don't get the wrong idea, Lana. I wasn't discriminating against your glasses."

"Y-you weren't…? Well, that's all right, then."

"I was discriminating against *you*."

"Why—yoooooou!"

Lana was about to put up her dukes when a mild voice from the back of the truck stopped her. "Yeeeesh. Quit fighting."

"B-but, Sonia! Pamela's being a jerk! She won't come up with one single plan of her own, and then she nitpicks mine!"

"There *are* no alternatives for those bizarro schemes of yours."

"Gwargh… Y-you…"

"I saaaid quit fighting."

Sonia looked several years younger than the other two. She was wearing an army helmet for some reason and was resting her chin on the sill of the window at the back of the cab. Her laid-back mediation seemed to have been effective: Pamela and Lana turned away from each other in a huff, but the conversation went on, minus the arguing.

"I'll go along with you on this. For now. I really don't want a repeat of that time at the museum last year, though."

"That wasn't my fault! It was that weird mummy couple or whatever they were! If we ever see them again, I'll thrash 'em good and shoot out their arms and legs three times each!"

"Don't. It's a waste of bullets," Pamela told her blandly.

"Say, Pamelaaa?" Sonia chirped from behind them. "Will we get to shoot lots of guns on this jooob?"

"…Well, hopefully we won't need to. If it happens, though, we're counting on you, Sonia."

"Yaaay!"

Although the three of them were talking like sisters, the conversation wasn't exactly a nice, sisterly chat. That was only natural.

"So about this job. Nobody normal would ever think up a thing like this."

"Huh?"

"Three women…trying to pull a train robbery."

It was only natural because they were a gang of three female robbers.

They went by the name "Vanishing Bunny."

Skimming over the particulars—as fans of the famous bandit Myra Belle (aka Belle Starr), the trio of young women was traveling around the States committing robberies.

Most of these jobs didn't count as real robberies, such as stealing small amounts of produce from fields. When they did attempt the occasional big heist, they'd invariably get hit with a stroke of rotten luck and wind up in a shoot-out with the police or the mafia. They were tragic heroines of their own making.

That said, having muddled through multiple firefights with police squads and the mafia, they seemed to have the favor of Lady Karma Houdini, if not Lady Luck.

Their very worst crisis had happened when they'd stolen jewels from a museum exhibit and were on their way out. For some reason, the doors had vanished, and a crowd had formed outside. Worse, some members of that crowd were police officers.

From what they'd heard later, the doors had been stolen by a man and woman who were wrapped in bandages from head to foot like mummies. The crowd of onlookers had believed it was some sort of publicity stunt.

When Vanishing Bunny had emerged later, they'd been mistaken for accomplices. Not only had the law gotten a good look at their faces, but the cops had chased them around for two whole weeks.

"I really thought our number was up that time. Just the police would have been bad enough, but the mafia, too?" Pamela forced a smile, breaking out in a cold sweat.

Lana huffed in annoyance. "That museum door had *sweethearts forever* graffiti carved into it by a mafia don and his first love… Seriously, how is that our problem?! How was *any* of that our problem?! I wish they'd take their complaints to that mummy couple!"

"Lana, calm dowwwn," Sonia chided in a voice that was as laidback as ever. There was no telling what she truly thought of that situation. She didn't sound angry or sad; she joined the conversation with nebulous confusion. "A museum, hmm…? Say, do you know what the train we're targeting is called?"

"No, I do not!"

Keeping one hand on the steering wheel, Pamela pressed her other hand to her temple. "…I wish you'd learned at least that, Lana. Since you're the one who suggested we rob this train, I would have loved if you knew anything at all about it…!" Promptly collecting herself, she turned to Sonia, acting as if Lana didn't even exist. "It's called the Flying Pussyfoot… It's famous. It has all these molded reliefs on both sides, like sculptures. People call it things like 'the rolling objet d'art' and 'the traveling museum.'"

"How about that…"

"If we get there and you still don't know what you're doing, Lana, I'll have to ask you if this is going to be okay again."

A train heist.

Yes, this had been a popular method of robbery since the days of the Old West, but how could three women pull one off? That was precisely what concerned Pamela.

"It's easy! We just have to stop the train while it's on the bridge! If it stops right in the middle, there won't be any way to leave it from the sides! Then we'll carefully take over the passenger cars, starting from the back…and that's the plan!" Lana said.

"…How are we going to stop the train?" Pamela asked.

"We can probably rig up gunpowder on the bridge and detonate it at some point, right?"

"There you go. Our failure is assured." Exasperated, Pamela pulled over to the shoulder and got out a map, intending to look for lodgings nearby.

"Wha—?! Wh-why are you giving up already?!"

"Relax, Lana. I gave up on you ages ago."

"Graaaaah! H-how dare you say that to me?! Hey, Sonia! You talk to her, too— Huh?" Lana turned around expecting to see Sonia, but her partner wasn't there.

In her place was a mountain of cargo. Hastily, Lana stuck her head through the window, scanning the bed—and spotted Sonia sleeping like a baby in the shadows of the luggage closest to the front.

"…Well, that's okay. You go on and sleep. We'll be staying up all night tonight, so you should sleep while you can."

"No, we're obviously going to find a hotel and take it easy," Pamela asserted.

"Just— Just wait a second! Hold on! I'll explain the brilliance of my plan in a hundred thousand words or less, starting now!"

Thirty minutes later

In the truck that was parked on the shoulder, Lana's sales pitch ran on for a while.

Lana and Pamela could hear quiet, drowsy breathing through the window that opened onto the truck bed, but neither the enthusiastic Lana nor her listener Pamela were paying attention to it.

In the end, Pamela compromised by agreeing to head to the scene and reopen their debate there, and they finally set off again.

"I swear… If we keep this up, who knows when we'll ever be millionaires."

"Don't you worry about that. Just leave it to me, and… Look, we'll even be able to live in a gorgeous mansion like that one over there!"

Lana superimposed her own future on the roof of the enormous mansion beyond the trees. Her eyes sparkled.

Pamela shook her head wearily and drove on without a word.

On the way to the highway, multiple cars passed them from behind. Pamela frowned. "I wonder if something happened. There are an awful lot of fast cars out today."

"They obviously don't belong to law-abiding citizens, so I bet there's a war on. Let's get out of here before we get dragged into it."

"Good idea," Pamela agreed. She stepped on the gas, heading away from Newark a bit faster than normal.

The rattletrap engine was still making a godawful racket thanks to its busted muffler, and so the women didn't notice the discrepancy until later when they were out of town.

In the bed of the truck, the peaceful breathing had gone from a solo to a duet.

Chapter 1　　　　**Dance with the Stray Rabbits**

December 30　　　Evening　　　Somewhere in New York

New York State is easy to say, but it takes more than a word or two to convey its vastness.

When people who aren't Americans hear *New York*, they usually only think about two things: the Statue of Liberty and Wall Street. Both are famous spots, one not far from Manhattan, and the other being on the island. Some probably think Manhattan is all there is to New York.

However, although population density is one thing, Manhattan is just a fraction of a fraction in terms of area. It's a part of New York City, which is itself only part of the state.

The current stage wasn't the heart of that glittering metropolis but a forested area far away from the big city.

The region was thickly wooded and usually deserted, but—

—at present, it was occupied by an oddly cheery group.

"All right, I'm gonna make sure we're all here! Sound off! One!"
"Two."
"Three."
"Four."
"Five." "Six." "Seven." "Eight." "Nine."

...

*　　　*　　　*

...

"Nineteen." "Twenty."

"Twenty-one."

"Twenty-two."

"Hya-haah!"

"Hya-haw!"

"Whoa, whoa! Hold it!" The guy who'd started the roll call put up both his hands, silencing the group.

He was still more of a boy than a "guy," really. On closer inspection, the men and women who stood around him all looked as if they were under twenty.

They certainly weren't well-dressed. If they'd been a little older, they might have been taken for workers who'd lost their jobs to the Depression and were drilling for a protest march. Most of them seemed like back-alley delinquents, though, and a few were clearly children.

Surrounded by those delinquents, the kid who'd been taking attendance shook his head. He pointed at one of the members of the group and called her out by name. "Chaini and Parrot, you gotta say the actual numbers. Gimme the numbers!"

The individual targeted by that accusatory finger looked confused. She was an Asian girl who wore thick glasses. "Hya-haah?"

"Hya-haw!"

Chaini tilted her head as she spoke, and the young boy beside her echoed her. It was like watching a pair of animals, and the delinquent kid hit them with a furious glare. "None of that 'Hya-haah' business! Get that outta here!"

"Hya-ya-ya-ya-ya-ya." "Hya-yaaw."

"Look, you guys, I'm serious! Jacuzzi's handed me a real important mission, a huge, once-in-a-lifetime job, and I absolutely can't blow it!" The boy crossed his arms as he lectured them.

The other delinquents exchanged looks.

"Wait, did Jacuzzi ask that guy specifically?"

"Noooo, he just did his usual vague thing and went around asking all of us."

"Yeah, figures."

"Actually, who is that guy?"

"Yeah, who are you?!"

"Who?! Who?!"

"Wait, I don't care who you are... I want money! Hand it over, bucko!"

"If you cough it up, I suppose I could do the roll call for you!"

"Hya-haah!" "Hya-haah." "Die." "Hya-haaaw!"

As everybody started shouting and jeering, the kid yelled back at them, temples twitching. "Hey, hold on a minute! One of you people just told me to die! Dammit, guys... Go to hell, you lousy jerks! Whoever said that is gonna die themselves! Okay, okay, okay, one of your number is on his way out... In a hundred— Yeah, inside of two hundred years, he's definitely gonna die!"

"Shaddup, punk!" "You're brattier than an actual brat!"

"Why'd you change it? Hey, why'd you switch from one hundred years to two hundred?"

"Because he figured we might make it to a hundred and fifteen or so!"

"He's a bigger worrywart than he looks!"

"Chicken! Chicken!"

"Hya-haah!" "Dieee."

"Wh-wh-wh-wh-wh-wh-wh-whyyyy, yooooou little—!"

The roll-calling delinquent screamed, his eyes tearing up under the concentrated onslaught, until a sound broke through the commotion.

Ding-ding-ding-ding-ding!

A bell echoed through the forest. On reflex, the delinquents turned to look in that direction.

"Okaaay. That's enough. You're wasting time. Time is dead."

"Melody..."

The girl who'd grabbed the delinquents' attention wore her blond hair tied up in two ponytails. She was holding the sort of handbells a shepherd would use, and she wore three watches on each arm; their design and quality were varied, and each one showed a different time.

Melody's eyes looked sleepy, and she spoke in an easygoing way. "That pointless exchange ate up eighty-three whole seconds of our valuable lives. Even as we speak, second by second, we're losing time. Even so, I've got a query—otherwise known as a question."

"W-well, spit it out."

"It's fine to do a sudden roll call, but we didn't call roll before we left. How is this going to tell us whether the whole group's here? That's what I want to know."

"......Oh."

It was an incredibly sensible question. All the delinquents, including the would-be leader, looked at one another.

"If that roll call itself was pointless, then the next time I say *seconds*, we'll have lost five hundred and eighteen seconds. If life ends at fifty years, each human is given 1,576,800,000 seconds. Taking a whole five hundred and thirty-six seconds of that teensy amount is a serious crime. Perhaps punishable by death. Think you can handle that? Come on, tell me—can you handle it? Here, feel the weight of five hundred seconds... That's five hundred seconds that aren't coming back, all right? Time that's past is death itself. Look, there, it'll be six hundred seconds soon."

Although her eyes were still sleepy, the girl with the watches tilted her head, coming closer.

"Whoa, wai— I—I'm sorry, all right?! We're square, yeah? Right?!" the boy shouted in a fluster.

"No. I can't forgive you. I've thought so for a while now, but both Jacuzzi and you people waste far too much time. If everybody's wasting time, my hobby won't be special anymore."

The girl's tone was suddenly serious.

The boy gulped. "...Hobby? Uh, remind me what your hobby was, Melody?"

"My hobby iiiis...wasting time."

"...Huh?"

"I know better than anyone how precious time is. That's exactly why I kill it proudly... I squash each second with affection, second by second. Everyone around me lives their life being pursued by the infinite demon of time, but I just watch them out of the corner of my eye, and I grind it under my heel. It's the ultimate entertainment. Looook, even as we speak, we've burned through six hundred and fifty seconds of today."

"I'm gonna knock you flat." Temples twitching, with an angry smile on his face, the boy hauled Melody up by her collar. That move earned him even more jeers from the gallery.

"He's gonna hit a girl!"

"He's not even a man! He's just scum!"

"Fellas like him go on to hit little kids!"

"Ghk... I'll step in for those future kids, slug you right now, and save us all some time!"

"Time is money... Time is money!"

"Why'd you say it twice?"

"That's how it is. And since I'm saving time, that means I get a dollar every time I slug you!"

The stuff his companions were saying was patently unfair, and the guy who'd called roll gave a shriek. "How does that even make sense?!"

"So who are you anyway?"

"You lousy no-good bags of—"

"Hya-haah!"

"Hya-haw."

"There, that's seven hundred seconds, gone forever," Melody said.

The conversation rambled on. It might as well have been lunchtime chatter. However, although they could have been campers, the group seemed terribly out of place in the woods.

As they chattered with one another, several of them thought back over the roles they'd been assigned.

⇔

A few days earlier   Somewhere in Chicago

Surrounded by the same group that was currently gathered in the woods, a kid with a tattoo of a sword on his face was giving a serious speech. "…And so, see, Nice and me and Donny and a few others are going to ride the Flying Pussyfoot, so I want the rest of you to take an earlier train and get there ahead of us."

"No!" "No." "Capital *N-O*!"

"Huh?! Wh-why not?!" Jacuzzi Splot stared at them in horror as they summarily derailed his speech. Tears welled up in his eyes.

"Oh, I just wanted to see how it felt to turn you down."

"That was mean!"

"Well, it's… Uh… When you're all confident, Jacuzzi, you just don't seem like you, so I figured we'd at least finish you off ourselves."

"Th-that makes no sense!"

Although he was apparently tough enough to get his face tattooed, Jacuzzi already looked ready to sob. Everyone around was fond of him and his timidity, though.

One of the kids turned to the side. "So, Miz Nice, once we pick up the goods, we'll move 'em out on our own say-so."

"Yes, if there's any left over, I'll dispose of it. Absolutely no open flames, and take care you don't drop any of it. I'd advise being a good distance away when we throw it into the river as well."

"Yeah, we know already."

The group was boisterously reviewing a certain plan. When you considered the details, it was only natural they'd be acting that way. This plan put not only their livelihoods but their very lives on the line.

The Flying Pussyfoot was a transcontinental express train. It was so luxurious that it was known as a rolling objet d'art, and they were planning to steal cargo that it would be secretly transporting.

Jacuzzi and Nice seemed to have their reasons, but most of the delinquents didn't give those much thought. They simply agreed to the maneuver in their own ways.

"So what are we stealing?"

Chatter resumed.

"They told us twenty-five seconds ago, and a hundred and twenty-three seconds ago. Get it through your thick skull already."

"Ah, sorry, I wasn't really listening."

"Nwah, steal, new bombs, Nice, happy."

"Bombs? Miz Nice already has a ton of those."

"But see, I hear this new kind packs five times the punch of a regular bomb."

"Five!"

"Hya-haah!"

"Hya-haw!"

"Hey, that'll bring in a bundle...!"

"Ngah, we can sell?"

"I've got this relative who wants to use explosives in a Hollywood movie."

"Although Nice probably just wants to blow 'em up."

"Well, that's it, then. Let's pitch in to make Miz Nice happy."

"I wanna go swimming in the river." "Are you nuts? It's December!"

"We can just warm it up with the explosives." "Oh yeah! You're a genius!"

"Actually, we're using 'em to blow the Russo Family to kingdom come, right?" "I like bombs, too. They're several years of destruction packed into a second."

"It's all about time with you, huh, Melody." "Well, time is the most familiar, trustworthy unit of measurement to her. Melody may have superimposed her own world over it and be experiencing life more deeply as a result." "Melody may be superimposed and deeply experienced!" "Hey, Chaini said something besides 'Hya-haah.'" "And Parrot still mimicked her...sort of." "It's been thirteen days, three hours, thirty-three minutes, and twenty-four seconds since the last time I heard Chaini say anything normal." "What, you keep track?!" "Don't spout random crap." "Well, it's true." "Okay then, if you're lying, you're gonna be my little sister!" "Gah-haaaw!" "Hya-haah!" "Geh-haaah!"

*　　*　　*

"Wh-whoa, whoa! Everybody, calm down!"

Jacuzzi clapped his hands, trying to get the chaos under control. Then the tension returned to his face. "Anyway, be careful. Somebody may call the cops on us right away, but if it comes to that, keep insisting you don't know me, and you'll be fine. If you tell them you just happened to be fishing in the river and picked that stuff up…"

"Hey, stupid, don't go talking hooey. If it was just you, it might be different, but you know we can't act like we don't know Miz Nice and Donny."

"H-huh? That was a mean thing to say, wasn't it?" Their perplexed leader didn't look happy about this.

The delinquents cackled at him, issuing warnings of their own.

"And hey, don't you go looking out a train window and spooking yourself, Jacuzzi. 'Waugh, there's no way this hunk of metal could actually move this fast!'"

"I—I'm not that much of a coward… B-but actually, it is pretty amazing that something that heavy can go so fast… If it hit you… W-waaaaaaaaaaaaaaaaaaaaaugh!"

Jacuzzi's face went white, and he backed up against the wall as he imagined getting struck head-on by a train.

Nice squeezed his hand gently. "It's all right, Jacuzzi. We're going to be *on* the train."

"I…I guess that's true, Nice. We'll be safe there, won't we?" Visibly relieved, Jacuzzi let his mind ruminate on the plan that was to take place a few days from now.

A mafia syndicate in New York had purchased a new type of bomb. If those bombs made it to their destination, New York would have a disaster on its hands. Jacuzzi had decided it would be safer to give the cargo to Nice or sell them to a construction site, and he had promptly resolved to steal them.

There was something else stirring in his heart, too. Deep down, he was still being careless.

Even if they were in third class, he thought he'd also get the experience of traveling on a luxury train.

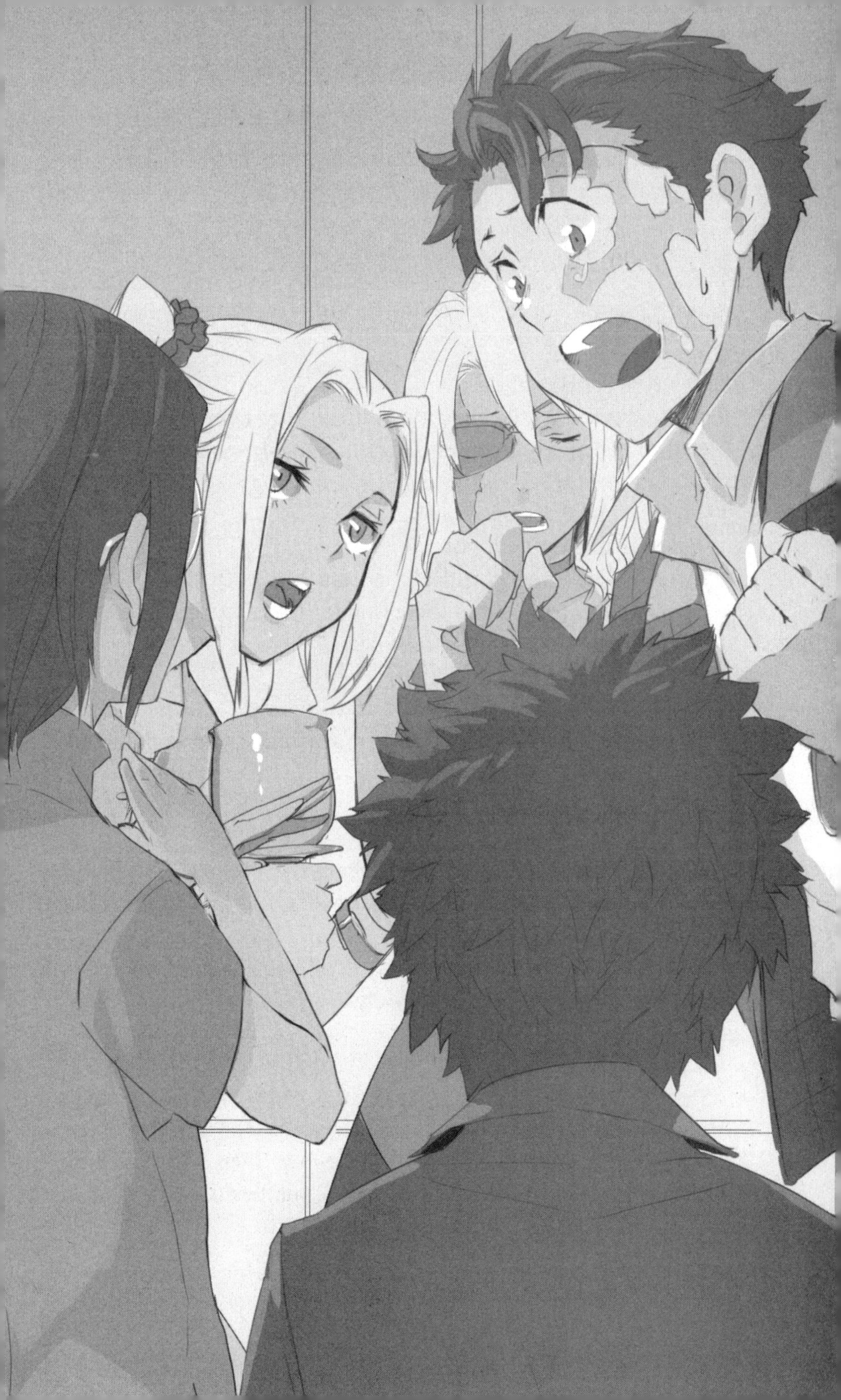

*   *   *

He had no idea what sort of trouble he'd find himself in once he stepped aboard.

⟺

In the woods

Back to the evening of the thirtieth...

Jacuzzi's group would be on the train already. Believing that their leader was currently living the high life, the delinquents reviewed their plan.

"So what are we gonna do next?"

"Help me find my little sister."

"Look, fella. You never had a little sister."

"Can't we just hang out in these woods until morning?"

"It's December!" "We'll freeze to death!"

"Eh, just don't sleep."

"Let's start a bonfire." "We can burn the forest."

"You idiot! We're retrieving bombs. That means no fire allowed, remember?!"

"*That's* the problem...?"

Keeping one eye on the guys as they rambled, Melody, Chaini, and the other girls were coolly checking the map and getting the situation straight in their minds.

"This is out of our control, but we don't know exactly when that train's going to pass through. If we get there late, the cargo will be swept downriver... We'll need time to launch the boats, too." Melody glanced at the two trucks parked behind them.

Some of the boys who were able to drive had borrowed the trucks from a nearby train station. Their beds were loaded up with several boats they'd borrowed from somewhere else. There was no telling what strings they'd pulled to get that loan, but they'd used one truck to carry the boats and the other to transport the group.

There were only five girls here. There were five times as many guys, and they wouldn't stop making a racket. However, as their surroundings got darker, their faces grew serious. One by one, they drifted over to the group of girls and began examining the map.

"Actually, we might freeze to death for real unless we do something. Whaddaya say? If you want us all to get in the truck and keep each other warm, I sure wouldn't min— Agh-guh-agh!"

Ignoring the kid who'd gotten his mouth plugged with some hard, stale bread, Melody nonchalantly pointed out a spot on the map. Her eyes still looked sleepy. "Let's see... There are a few bungalows for hunters to use in the summer right here. Let's use them. Somebody might already be there, but we might be able to borrow some fire and blankets. If nobody's beaten us to it, let's just stay there for ten hours."

⇔

Meanwhile Somewhere in New York State

While the gang of delinquents was deciding to head for the bungalows, not too far away, the truck carrying the gang of female bandits was stopped on the side of the road again.

"What's wrong? We're almost there, aren't we?"

The location Lana had chosen for their robbery of the Flying Pussyfoot was a bridge over a river halfway between New York City and the Great Lakes region. That bridge was long enough for their purpose, and they'd be able to flee in any direction they chose. If they got the money, they could even head straight for Canada.

Or so she'd thought, but since she'd settled on that spot without considering anything else, they wouldn't be able to do anything until they'd actually looked it over.

Once they'd reached that conclusion that afternoon, they'd forced their jalopy to carry them all the way here.

Pamela checked the meter, then shut off the engine. "We're running low on gas. We'll have to fill up soon."

Gas stations did exist at this point in history, but they hadn't spread all across the country yet. Many travelers filled barrels or oil drums with gasoline and took them along, and Pamela's group was no exception; they'd driven all around the country on the barrels of gas in the back of their truck.

"I'll check the map to see if there are any bungalows nearby. Would you gas up the truck?" Pamela was already unfolding the map.

Realizing the other woman had no intention of leaving the cab, Lana opened the door and *tsk*ed to herself. "Honestly. I need my brain for work. What if the gasoline fumes make me dumb?"

"You couldn't get any dumber, so don't worry about it."

"…I hope you drive right into a truck! Oh, wait, then I'd be in the wreck, too…," Lana grumbled.

Pamela watched her head outside and began impassively reading the map. There was a cluster of bungalows for summer hunters up ahead. If they did actually pull off this train robbery, it might not be a bad idea to use those as their base.

As Pamela marked the spot with a pencil, a shriek came from the back of the truck.

"Eeek!" It was Lana.

"…? What happened? Did you fall and soak yourself with gasoline? I could set you on fire and warm you up. Forever." She lobbed her sarcastic threat out the window, but Lana said nothing in response.

"…?"

Frowning, Pamela folded the map, climbed out of the cab, and turned around. Lana was peeking under the canvas canopy, her mouth flapping soundlessly.

"What's the matter?" Pamela said with an exaggerated sigh as she walked to the back of the truck. She peeked into the bed. "Is Sonia stark naked a…gain…?"

She froze just like Lana.

Before their eyes was an unfamiliar boy, blissfully snoozing away.

Zzzz… Zzzz… Zzzz…

⇔

Meanwhile　　In the woods

After the trucks carrying the gang of delinquents and their boats had driven away, the stone-faced men who had been watching them from a distance began whispering among themselves.

("...Are they gone?")

("What was that? They can't be campers, not at this time of year.")

("They probably came to do some dope or have an orgy. Guess the cold got the better of them and they headed home.")

The men, who were wearing military uniforms, turned back and headed deeper into the woods. Their expressions were still set.

("Let's return to camp. The operation begins in another two hours.")

("Yes, sir!")

The men walked in silence—except for the man who appeared to be their leader. "Let us hope the negotiations succeed on the first attempt," he murmured with a thin smile.

"It may be for the sake of the revolution...but even *I* don't want Comrade Goose to put a bullet through a child's skull."

And so they headed for the bridge.

They were a unit of the Lemures, a revolutionary terrorist group. Their role was to negotiate and relay the results to their comrades on the Flying Pussyfoot.

The maneuver involved taking a senator's wife and daughter hostage—practically a suicide mission. However, none of them had the slightest suspicion that Goose and their comrades might fail.

This was completely understandable.

After all, they had no way of knowing exactly *what* was on that train with them.

⇔

In the back of Vanishing Bunny's truck

"Let me ask you again: What's your name?"

"Carzelio… Carzelio Runorata."

"Okay, I'm calling you Cazze. Cazze, when did you get into our truck?"

"I'm sorry… Um…" The boy lowered his eyes apologetically.

Pamela gently stroked his hair to reassure him. "Don't worry. We're not mad. We were just a little startled. That's all."

"Th-thank you… I ran away from home… The truck was right there, so I got in and hid so they wouldn't take me back…"

"I see… Still, it's lucky you didn't fall right out, napping in the bed like that. Sonia, keep him company for a while."

"Nyergl?" Hearing her name, Sonia sputtered from the back of the truck's bed. Her eyes were hazy with sleep. She'd been awake for a little while, but she wasn't fully alert yet, and she still didn't seem to know what was going on.

Leaving Cazze in her care, Pamela stepped away from the truck and took Lana with her.

"He probably climbed in right after Sonia fell asleep," Pamela said once they had some distance from the truck, calmly assessing the situation.

The boy's clothes were muddy in places, but they were clearly different from what normal children wore. There was something peculiar about them; even an amateur could tell they weren't clothes most kids would be wearing. Whoever dressed him wanted him to be in luxury.

If they'd been told the boy was a descendant of English nobility, they would have believed it from the way he carried himself. Lana's eyes were glittering, but Pamela sighed, frowning. "Who'd have thought we'd pick up a runaway?"

"…With clothes like his, he's got to be from that incredible mansion. I bet his jacket alone cost what a midlevel bank clerk would make in a week. Maybe even a whole month."

Pangs of jealousy nipped at Pamela as she remembered the mansion Lana had pointed out that afternoon. "What do you suppose he had to run away from, living in such a nice house?" However, she still believed rich people had worries of their own, so she didn't make any bitter comments about him. *Besides, we're bandits. We can't exactly talk.* Inwardly, Pamela scoffed.

Meanwhile, Lana clapped her hands together lightly, spectacles gleaming. "I just had a brilliant idea! Let's kidnap him and collect a ransom!"

"You say that like it's easy... Frankly, I considered it myself, but..." Pamela clicked her tongue, embarrassed to have had the same idea as Lana even briefly. After a short pause to think, she agreed—on one condition. "It seems like a better plan than robbing the train... but let's make sure the boy never realizes he's been kidnapped. I don't want to deal with scaring him off and chasing him down, and I don't want to traumatize the poor kid."

"Why not just shoot him in the leg?"

"...Are you serious?"

"I'm kidding, of course."

Pamela gave her an icy glare, and Lana averted her eyes, breaking out in a cold sweat.

Meanwhile, Pamela had an odd sense that something wasn't quite right. "Still, 'Runorata'...," she murmured. "I've heard that name before..."

"Well, duh. They're rich people who live in a humongous house. I bet we've heard their name on the radio or seen it in the papers, and we just didn't care enough to remember anything else."

"...You think?"

Pamela didn't feel entirely convinced. That said, she couldn't remember anything else, so she kept the vague, unsettled feeling to herself.

"Yaaaay, how cuuute! You look just like Nader when he was a kiiid."

"P-please don't do that. Who's Nader?"

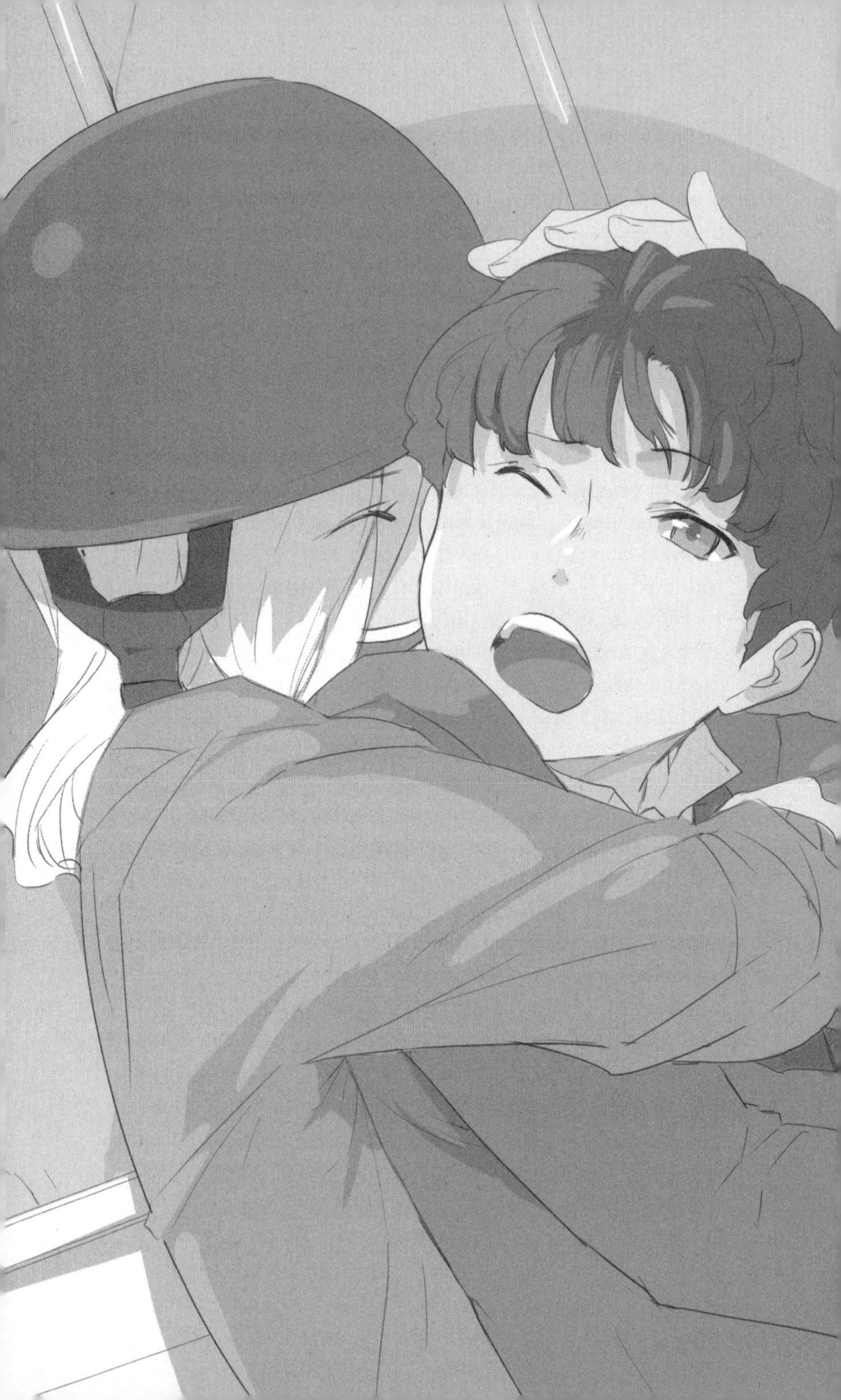

When the two of them returned to the back of the truck, they found Sonia petting Cazze's head like a cat. He was blushing bright red.

Lana spoke to him with a friendly smile. "Say, Cazze? Do you know the telephone number for your house?"

"Huh?! U-um… Are you going to call them?"

"Oh, don't worry! We're not going to tell them to come get you. We just… Well, if you up and disappear, your people will worry, you know? We thought we'd give them a ring and tell them you were fine. You're planning to go home tomorrow either way, right?"

Lana smiled brightly, adjusting her glasses. Cazze hesitated. However, deciding the three women could be trusted, he obediently told them his home telephone number.

As a result, they attracted another piece of the impending ruckus.

⟺

The outskirts of Newark   In the Runorata mansion

I'll be back by the New Year. Don't worry. It isn't anybody's fault, so please don't be mad at them.

When he was informed that his first grandchild had written a note and disappeared, Bartolo Runorata sighed, frowning. "Hmm… Well, I'd imagine this life is hard on a boy his age."

The boss of the Runorata Family was a bit over fifty. The wrinkles on his dignified face were neither particularly shallow nor deep, and his spectacles made him look intellectual.

"Still, he's got more gumption than I thought. That's good," he murmured.

"This is no time to be saying that, boss!" Cazze's father shouted. "He's— He genuinely doesn't know what it's like out there!! He has no idea what sort of dangers there are!"

"But it was you two who raised him that way."

"Ngh…!"

Bartolo didn't interfere with his grandson's education any more than he had to. He'd taught him the manners that were appropriate for his age, but as a rule, he respected his daughter's and son-in-law's opinions. Although he'd expressed a few doubts about keeping the boy so extremely sheltered and never letting him go outside by himself, he'd ultimately let the child's parents decide how to handle things.

Granted, I doubt I'll have any part to play in this affair.

His son-in-law's men were searching desperately, but Bartolo didn't intend to dispatch any more of the Family's members than he had to. This wasn't because he wasn't concerned for his grandson. He didn't want to cause a big fuss and risk alerting other Families.

This incident isn't in our jurisdiction yet.

He was worried, but on the other hand, he knew how the boy felt. He didn't think that dragging him back against his will would be the right move. As far as Bartolo was concerned, sending guards to shadow him secretly once they found him would be enough.

In stark contrast to Bartolo, Cazze's father was clearly anxious. He pointed at the men in charge of guarding Cazze, who were standing nearby, and shouted, "If you'd been keeping a proper eye on him, this never would have—"

"Put your finger down."

"……!"

Bartolo's words held a quiet pressure, and everyone around him swallowed hard.

"No, boss. He's right. It is all my fault."

"That's not for you to decide." The guard seemed liable to offer to kill himself at any moment, and Bartolo spoke to him quietly. "When Cazze comes back, learning his helpers have been punished would come as a shock. If you've lost all your fingers as a result of his little excursion…"

"……!"

Everyone understood that he wasn't speaking hypothetically. Even Cazze's father felt cold sweat break out on his back.

The situation was stagnant, and just as an unpleasant silence threatened to dominate the room, a butler-esque man came over and whispered something in Bartolo's ear.

"Well, well..." Bartolo's eyebrows twitched slightly. Showing no emotion, he quietly rose from his chair.

"Boss...? What is it?" His behavior seemed to worry Cazze's father; his expression was uneasy.

Bartolo's next words were as impassive as ever. "I'm told there's been a phone call demanding a ransom."

"Huh...?"

"We've been ordered to bring cash to a designated bungalow by tomorrow morning, without informing the police. They're more frightened of the police than they are of us. That's quite a joke."

"N-n-no! It can't be! Ca...Cazze has been kidnapped?!" The man's face had gone white as a sheet.

"It appears that, *finally*, the matter has come under our jurisdiction." Bartolo was unflappable.

"In that case...all I need to do is issue orders to the appropriate people."

⟺

A few minutes later—

Two military motorcycles sped away from the Runorata Family's mansion.

The bikes had been heavily modded, and they raced down the dark road at a speed that easily surpassed thirty miles per hour.

The riders were dressed as if they'd slipped out of a party, in sharp swallowtail coats and shiny patent leather shoes, and they were identical twins. They wore goggles over their indistinguishable faces, which had no expression on them whatsoever.

Just as the bikes hit their top speed, they shifted to ride side by side as smoothly as if they'd planned it. In perfect sync, their lips curved into smiles.

The twins were guards who worked directly for Bartolo himself, and even in the Runorata mansion, they hardly ever spoke to anyone except him or each other. This was the first "hunt" they'd been assigned in a long time, and the thought of the mission made their hearts leap.

At the exact same moment, they opened their mouths, and an odd song began to echo between the two of them.

♪ Come, let's begin the hunt.
Swing your blade; drive your prey before you.
Run twisterly, wavagly, loppely.
Don't overtake it, even when it's in your grasp.
Don't let it escape, even when it's slipping away.
Run swiftig, stumblect, dronkily.
When the rabbit is tired, raise your blade.
The little rabbit is spent.
The strength is yours. The kill is yours.
What you need are courage and hope.
Kill that exhausted rabbit.
First kill the rabbit, next kill a pig.
Take the pig's head, then take a deer's.
Until a man or a monster awaits you.
Large or small, array yourselves
before us, blessings of the land.
Cut them apart bravely.
Be greedy, be grateful.
Come, let's begin the hunt. ♪

Singing like children headed out on a hike, they raced through the darkness as if they were enjoying themselves enormously, keeping their bikes at top speed.

The noise of their engines and the wind drowned out their voices.

Although they were zipping down the road side by side, their song didn't even reach their own ears.

Even so, they went on singing at the exact same speed and in the exact same rhythm.

They almost seemed to be announcing the beginning of the impending ruckus...

Digression

"Hey, hey, Isaac?"

"What is it, Miria?!"

"Have you ever seen a circus?"

"Of course I have! I went to the circus when I was a kid. Just once! I think!"

"You 'think'?"

"Well, I remember there were all sorts of animals doing all manner of who-knows-what, but I can't remember if it was a circus or a zoo. But that's peanuts, my dear; don't worry about it!"

"Done and done!"

"So what about the zoo, Miria?"

"You mean the circus, Isaac. Um, well, Firo says his friend used to be in a circus! He says he can walk a tightrope and jump through a flaming hoop and throw knives—and that's just the beginning!"

"Amazing! I'd expect no less from Firo!"

"Firo's amazing?"

"Of course he is! Having friends with those extraordinary talents means you can learn how to walk a tightrope anytime. So if Firo set his mind to it, he could walk a tightrope or jump through a flaming hoop whenever he wanted! If we threw knives at him, I know he'd be able to catch them in an apple on his head!"

"Woooow!"

Alveare was the same as always, including Isaac and Miria's conversation. And Firo's protests.

"What the hell are you saying?!" he shouted, exasperated.

Isaac's and Miria's eyes widened in surprise. "What?! You're not amazing, Firo?"

"You're not?"

"It's not a question of whether I'm amazing, all right...?" Firo gave them a thousand-yard stare.

Isaac and Miria responded with smiles. "Don't worry about it, Firo! You don't have to be amazing; Miria and I like you just fine!"

"Yes, it's amazing that you're *not* amazing! You're the cat's pajamas, Firo!"

"...Uh, yeah, well, I'll take the goodwill at face value," Firo said, now fully lost.

From behind him, Ennis joined the conversation. "The circus...?" She was a homunculus, created by alchemy, who also happened to be a friend of theirs.

"Oh, you interested in that stuff, too, Ennis?" Firo asked.

"I was just wondering: Does everyone enjoy those sorts of things?" she asked with surprising gravitas.

"Huh?" Firo stared.

"I'm sorry, Firo. I know the word, but I have no 'memories' of actually seeing a circus, so I can't really imagine what it's like... What about it is enjoyable?"

"Oh, uh... It's, well... Good question." Her earnest inquiry had taken him off guard.

His boss, Maiza Avaro, had been listening in from a seat at the counter, and he threw Firo a lifeline. "I imagine a big part of the appeal is seeing someone overcome the limits you'd always believed in."

"What do you mean, limits?"

"Well, first-rate acrobats and trained animals go beyond the limitations we assume humans have. There's a certain exhilaration in seeing something truly new and unknown."

"Oh… Yeah, you're right. Say someone shows you the biggest pumpkin you've ever seen—you'd probably go 'Whoooooa!' or somethin'."

Expanding on Firo's example, Maiza continued. "Yes, when they see something that far surpasses their expectations, humans often exclaim in wonder. Or in fear."

"Yeah, when it's a bug that's too damn big, what you feel sure isn't wonder…," said Firo.

From behind the counter, the restaurant's proprietor spoke up. "All right, fellas, don't start talking about giant bugs in a restaurant. You'll have the customers thinking about cockroaches!"

"Please don't say that so loudly, Miz Seina!"

"Why do you suppose people loathe cockroaches so much?"

"Ennis! She just said not to talk about it!"

As they watched Firo and the others get noisy, Isaac and Miria went on with their own discussion.

"Hmm. I don't really get it, but I guess he means the bigger, the more impressive! Or scary!"

"Yes, that's amazing! And scary!"

"If you got as big as a building, Miria, I think I'd be more impressed than scared!"

"Really? Yaaay! Thank you, Isaac!"

The two had vanished into their own private world, but Firo had overheard them. "…The scariest thing to me is how simple your brains are," he said.

"Not that I really mind it."

Interlude

December 29, 1931   Noon

While Jacuzzi's friends were still in Chicago and Cazze was studying quietly in the Runorata mansion, a child was playing alone in a forest in upstate New York.

His parents had told him he mustn't ever go in there by himself.

There was a river a ways in, an iron railroad bridge over the river, and a road that led all the way to that bridge. The forest wasn't really deep enough for people to get trapped in.

However, woods were woods. You could never get careless in them. The boy's parents had grown up hearing that from their families as well. He had come here anyway.

He was here to prove he was old enough to walk through those dangerous woods. In short, it was a test of courage.

He hadn't been threatened by local bullies, and he hadn't made a bet with his friends. He'd stepped inside the woods voluntarily.

There were no signs of coyotes, wolves, or wild boars, and as he ran around in the woods, he felt vaguely disappointed.

Had he been an adult, he probably would have picked up on the fact that the situation was already abnormal.

No coyotes, no wolves, no boars, no deer or dogs or wild rabbits— even for winter, the animals were far too scarce.

That was why the boy saw it—something that had remained in the forest. Something he should never have seen.

He saw *him*.

It wasn't as if the boy had had a close encounter.

From a great distance—so far away that the boy's eyes could only barely make him out—there *he* was.

The boy was standing far, far, far away, somewhere safe, but the sight still paralyzed him. He started to hear a strange clicking, gnashing sound. He didn't realize it was the sound of his own chattering teeth.

His figure was just that overwhelming.

Even though *he* looked no bigger than the little bugs that were flying around near the boy, the boy understood just how fearsome *he* was. His own instincts made him understand it, almost compulsively.

Abruptly, *he* turned his head in the boy's direction.

At that, the kid bolted like a rabbit.

It took only a few minutes to get away, but to him, it felt like ten years.

He didn't know how he'd fled or what path he'd taken. The next thing he knew, he was in front of his own house.

He didn't tell anyone about it. He just crawled into bed, pulled the covers up over his head, and shivered.

The boy was hoping what he'd seen had been a dream.

There was nothing else he could do.

Chapter 2   The Rabbits Huddle Close in the Darkness

The kids didn't have anywhere to go.

Each of them had lost their place for a different reason. Some of their histories would provoke sympathy from strangers. Other events were completely and totally their fault. Still more were a comical product of coincidence.

Put another way, the reasons didn't matter at all.

These children with nowhere to go drifted, carried along by the mood in the streets. They were led astray by strangers' voices, and at last, like dead leaves in the wind, they *accumulated* in several different places.

This particular place was merely one such haunt.

If there was a difference between this and any other group, it was that there was a little sack in the middle of the drift.

The sack could hold an infinite quantity of dead leaves. It was thin and unreliable, but it would never, ever tear.

If Jacuzzi Splot had anything going for him, it was a kind of "personal magnetism."

He was cowardly enough for two, and yet the things he did were truly fearless. In Chicago, he'd gotten involved with bootlegging and squared up with the Russo Family. Eight of his friends had been bumped off as "examples." Any normal person would have gotten cold feet and backed off or acted on their rage and gone down fighting.

The kids who gathered around Jacuzzi were not normal.

They attacked multiple Russo Family speakeasies and high-interest moneylenders simultaneously, causing enough damage to crack their opponents' foundation.

Not one member of their group backed out. Nobody opposed the move.

It wasn't because Jacuzzi had power. He didn't have the sort of charisma that made people serve him. He hadn't done them any special favors.

At the end of the day, the kids who gravitated to him had a vague, instinctive understanding that this crybaby was probably their very last bastion.

Jacuzzi was the one who'd taken them in and made a place for them when they were being swept along helplessly, who'd saved them from being lost forever in the current—who cared about them.

If they lost him, they knew they would be trampled into a road somewhere, like dead leaves.

Somewhere along the way, they'd become an unruly mob, a murder of crows—and a very tight-knit group.

Sometimes they even ripped out the throats of wolves.

Other kids with nowhere to go drifted in, one by one. By now, they had enough power to rival a modest gang. They were constantly growing.

Whether Jacuzzi wanted that was another matter.

⇔

Night   Somewhere in the forest   The bungalows

Ding-ding-ding-ding!

A sound that was out of place in the winter woods rang out, followed by Melody's clear voice. "Okay, all right. Gather 'round. Everyone, get over here in roughly twenty-eight seconds."

A vast forest spread around them, and there were scattered patches of lingering snow left over from the other day. A line of several large bungalows stood beside the road that ran through the trees. They'd been built for the hunting season and were waiting quietly for their intended users, the hunters.

That's how it should have been, at least.

A group of more than twenty boys and girls had gathered in front of the biggest bungalow. They'd assembled around the girl with the bells, and they were all saying whatever they wanted.

"'Roughly' and 'twenty-eight seconds'? Look, Melody…"

"Why are you the one running the show?"

"Meh, it doesn't matter who runs it."

"Then why not me, huh?"

"Nah, you're the one person who can't."

"Why not?!"

"…Because I hate your guts…"

"Don't just tell me to my face! Haven't you ever heard of passive aggression?! Just getting the brush-off would be better!"

"Yo, it's cold. Let's get inside."

"Hey, should we really be using these without asking anybody?"

"Not like there's anything in there to steal. Nobody's gonna mind if we use 'em to keep out of the cold."

"If we keep from starving, too, that'll be perfect."

"If my little sister's in there, *that* would be perfect."

"What the heck?"

"Hya-haah!"

"Hang on a second, I just got hungry."

"Who cares, dumbbell?"

"I wonder if we could eat the wall or something."

"What are you even talking about?!"

"Well, this shack is made out of wood, right? Wood's a plant. Don't that mean you can eat it?"

"I hear you can if you stew it with tiger fat."

"Tiger fat?"

"You mean butter?"

"The ones that ran around and around the tree?"

"I see… Yeah, trees and tigers do seem real tight with each other."

"No they ain't."

"Hya-haah!" "Hya-haw!"

Chaos.

The conversation was sheer chaos.

It meant nothing. The strings of words existed just to assert the fact that these people were here. However, they seemed to be having a whole lot of fun. In the middle of the desolate forest, they were casting their own protective barrier.

Waiting until exactly twenty-eight seconds had passed since she'd first spoken, Melody rang her bells again.

Ding-ding-ding-ding!

"All right, quiet. Quiet down. So now we need to kill time until tomorrow morning..." At that, Melody's sleepy eyes softened and began to sparkle. "Ahhh... Killing time... That's suuuch a great phrase. Our lives are dominated by time, and yet we're going to kill it. What amazing, phenomenal luxury! In a way, being able to waste time is much, much more extravagant than wasting money."

"Y-you think?" One of the guys cocked his head.

Melody nodded, wearing a rapturous smile. "Of course! After all, you're wasting time from your own limited life, you know? You could actually say you were wasting your life! Eeee, the luxury!"

"It sounds like something no one would ever praise you for."

"If you want compliments, you can't be extravagant. Oh, we'll have to kill time with all our might! We're wasting time right now! We all need to hurry and kill time together!"

Melody bounced with excitement, ringing her bells.

The delinquent looked even more puzzled. "Sometimes I can't tell whether you're a genius or an idiot."

At that, the kids around him all jumped into the conversation at once. "What, you don't even know that? You sure are dumb, fella!"

"I can tell... Hey, Melody. What's thirty-five plus twenty-six?"

"Huh? Sixty-one?"

"Whoa... She managed to add double digits... She's smarter'n you anyway!"

"Yeah, at the very least, you ain't got no right to call Melody dumb."

"Hya-haah!"

"Hya-haw!"

"Wh—! Hey! Don't just shove your oars in! You think I can't add double digits?! Like hell I can't!"

"It's fine. Don't push yourself."

"Gnrrrrrrrrrrgh!"

As the conversation began to wander off, Melody's bells rang again. *Ding-ding-ding-ding.* The girl with sleepy eyes spun around in time to the rhythm. Around and around, this way and that.

She was performing a musical all by herself, with the woods as her stage.

"...What's the dance for, Melody?" asked one of the delinquents.

"Search me. I randomly danced to kill time, that's all!" For some reason, Melody puffed out her chest proudly.

The delinquent clutched his head, groaning loudly. "...Look, let's have a conversation that actually means something, okay?! I'm begging you people!"

"What meaning? We're killing time until tomorrow morning. Therefore, anything we do while we're waiting has meaning, you see? The super-important meaning that we're waiting! Ooh, how splendid! We're killing time meaningfully! We'll kill time and get praised for it. How extravagant!"

"Dammit... One of these days, you're gonna regret all the time you've wasted." Grumbling, the delinquent scanned the area. He seemed to have been in a fight at one point; his upper front teeth were neatly broken.

Once again, he registered how cold the woods were.

Part of it was the lack of human presence, but the climate in this area was also chillier than the one back home in Chicago. It was so cold that the fact that there wasn't much snow here in the dead of winter was unusual.

"Well, whatever. Let's hurry up and get inside. We're gonna freeze out here."

At that remark from the kid with missing teeth, the group began funneling into the hut.

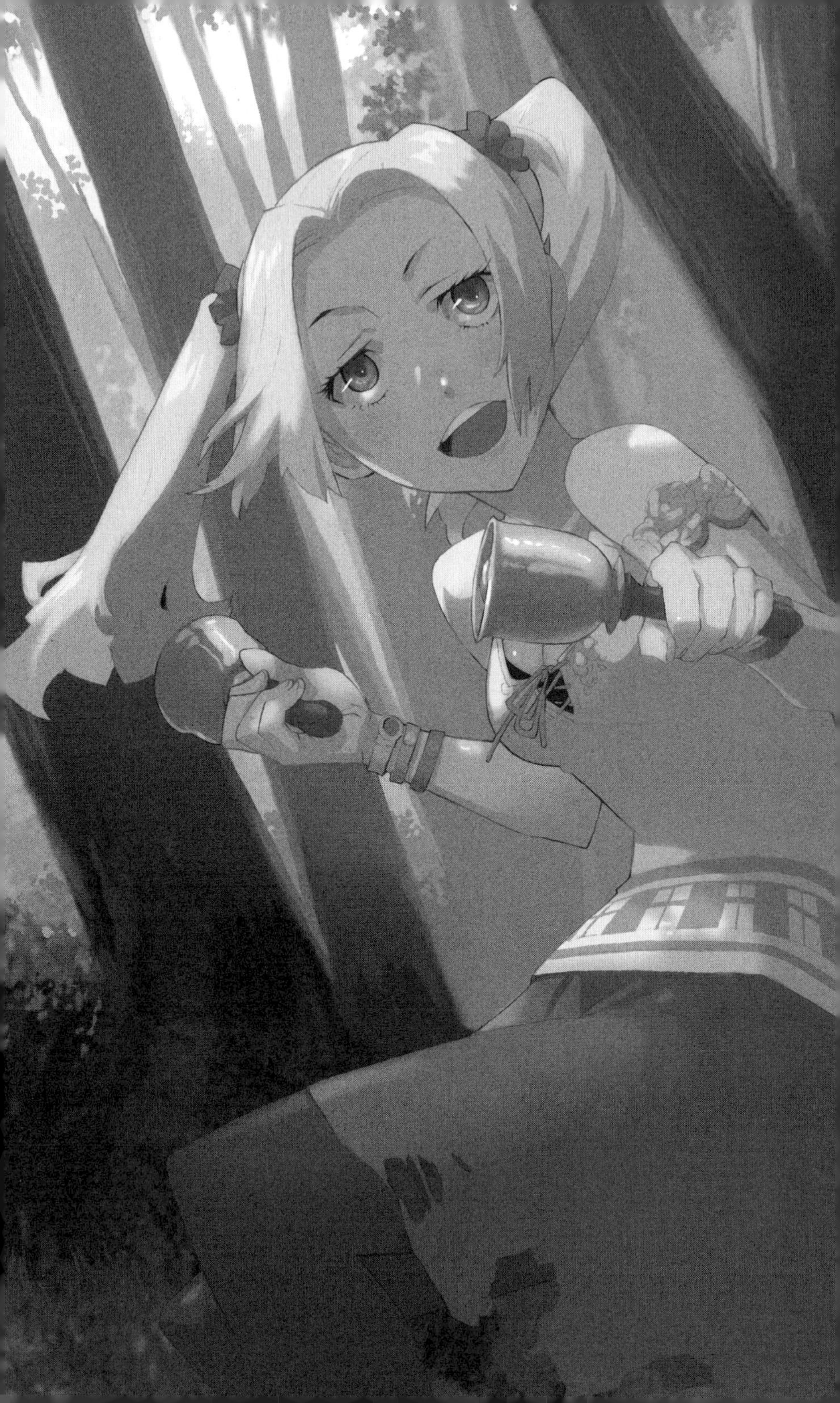

However, Melody gazed at the road that ran past the bungalows, tilting her head.

"What's up, Mel?" one of the group's few girls called to her.

Melody rang a bell, just once, and narrowed her eyes. "Mm... I was thinking there were an awful lot of tire tracks here."

"Huh?" "Hya-haw?"

"This doesn't seem like a place that normally gets a lot of traffic... Well, I guess it doesn't matter."

Deciding there was no sense in giving it too much thought, Melody headed inside. Looking at the excessive number of watches she wore on both arms, she smiled happily and thought of the time they were about to waste. "Now as long as nobody comes by in the next thirteen hours, twenty-one minutes, and fifty-three seconds, we'll be set."

All they had to do was kill time. Nothing more. That being the case, they didn't bother to check all the bungalows carefully.

Oblivious to what lurked inside the one farthest from theirs, the young delinquents got started on their long night.

⇔

Bungalow Number 7

He really shouldn't have been there.

In some ways, *he* was a being that should not have been at all.

This area wasn't his home.

That was much farther west, in northwestern California.

He hadn't seen his family in a very long time.

He'd been separated from them when *he* was small.

Incidentally, *he* didn't know there was no one who remotely resembled him, let alone his family, in this entire region.

Conversely, humans probably couldn't tell what *he* was thinking.

In simple terms of what *he* was doing at the moment, *he* was asleep, breathing peacefully in the bungalow that was farthest from the one Melody and the others had gone into—with an enormous quantity of food piled in front of him.

There were other things *he* didn't know.

He should technically already have shoveled that food into his belly and fallen into a long, long sleep, until spring came.

Of the species that resembled them, *his kind* did tend to be shallow sleepers as a rule. However.

Something had disturbed his instincts, and *he* couldn't settle into that long sleep.

He just kept on eating, driven by some unknown need.

Was it the cold winter temperatures, or because *he* was indoors?

The smell of his meals was barely detectable outside.

As a result, no one had noticed him there.

Not even now.

While *he* dozed, though, several sounds had reached him.

The peal of bells, loud but light, and something *he'd* heard until just a little while ago: the clamor of young human voices.

Had something about those noises struck him as nostalgic, or had it been some other instinct?

Even though night had all but fallen, his mind was gradually warming up and moving toward wakefulness.

Slowly, slowly…

⟺

Bungalow Number 1

The bungalow the group of delinquents had chosen hadn't even been locked, and it was nearly empty inside.

There was nothing fancy about it: It was just a big, empty space, plunked down by the roadside.

It didn't really belong to anybody. It might have been built by a few hunters on public land. In that case, if they claimed they'd gotten stranded and found the place, no one would mind if they warmed up there without permission.

That said, only a couple of them were actually thinking about things like that. The rest just started to make themselves at home.

"Man, there's really nothing here, huh?"

"That means there's lots of space. That's good."

"I haven't bunked on a floor with this much room since I slept outside."

"Now if we just had some blankets."

"Blankets, and also food."

"And steak. Gimme steak."

"Gimme money."

"Gimme a little sister."

"Hya-haw."

The delinquents lazed on the floor wherever they wanted, saying whatever they liked. They stayed fully dressed, stretching their limbs, not seeming to care that their backs would get dirty.

The girls strode between the guys on the floor, discovered that there were several beds in an inner room on the other side of a wall, and exchanged high fives.

There were no sheets, but if they brought in the blankets they'd packed in the truck with the boats, they'd have proper bedding. Getting right to work, Melody and the other girls returned to the big room where the guys lay around like kittens.

The calm atmosphere came to an abrupt end as a boy who'd been looking out a window near the entrance turned back to them. "Somebody just drove up."

"Huh?"

"What is it?"

"Shoot, maybe it's whoever owns this place."

"No, I bet it's my little sister."

"Oh, shaddup."

"Listen up, the story is that we're here because we got stranded. Got it?"

"...Even though our trucks are parked right outside?"

"Aaaaah! Dammit!"

Ignoring his confused friends, the guy who'd first made the discovery went on providing commentary. It was already dark outside, but the light by the bungalow's entrance illuminated a vehicle that had stopped right behind their truck.

"What the hell? That's one ratty old tin can... Aw man, it stopped right by our truck. And it's carrying... Uh...? Whoa! This hot tomato just got out!"

When they heard that, the boys all got excited.

"It's my little sister!"

"She's older'n you."

"You idiot! Age doesn't matter for little sisters!"

"It does, too!"

"Sorry, pal, that's not your little sister—that's my girl. What's she doing all the way out here?"

"......? ...! Dammit! You had me going for a second there!"

"Even if she was your girl, she could still be my little sister! No contradictions there!"

"Well, I mean, you ain't wrong, but..."

"And also, I'm not giving my little sister to you!"

"What was that, you skunk?!"

"Hya-haah!" "Hya-haw."

The boys were gearing up for a fight over something stupid when, outside the window, the situation changed again.

The first one to get out of the truck had been a woman with a ponytail. She'd apparently been driving, and she was wearing a light jacket.

Next, a bespectacled young woman appeared from the passenger seat, and a girl who was a bit younger emerged from the back of the truck. Finally, a boy climbed out; he was wearing very nice clothes, and he might not have been ten years old yet. The group began to discuss something; they were examining the delinquents' trucks.

"Hey, they're all dolls," a boy said, whistling.

The usual suspect clenched his fists and spoke up: "They're all my little sisters!"

"...I think that last kid was a boy."

"He'll be my little brother, then!"

"What, that's okay?!"

"I just— I just want a family!"

"C'mon, ya blockhead! We're already family!"

"......! You jerk... Are you trying to make me cry?!"

Behind the guys who were having that emotional exchange, the delinquent with the missing front teeth had a twitch in his face. "You're all ridiculous."

Chapter 3 Bunny & Honey

Lana was the one who'd named the gang of bandits "Vanishing Bunny."

The trio hadn't been called anything at first, until she randomly started introducing themselves by that name. Although whenever she tried to introduce them to someone else at all, Pamela invariably strangled her.

Pamela had neither agreed to nor actively rejected the name, while Sonia had smiled and said, "A bunny? Cute."

Lana had begun as a petty luggage thief who worked alone. Some vicious men had caught her once and would have killed her if Pamela hadn't been passing by and rescued her. After that, the two women had teamed up.

Pamela had started out as a gambler traveling around provincial underground casinos—although she'd actually been stealing money from them.

Their personalities were polar opposites, yet they got along oddly well. They went all over the country together, committing a string of minor heists at underground casinos and betting shops, but as they were passing through the wilderness, they'd found an odd little girl firing guns over and over.

The girl had introduced herself as Sonia. There was a horse-drawn wagon loaded with dozens of guns beside her. "They're mementos of my parents," she'd said, still firing all the while. Without ever making a formal decision, Pamela and Lana had taken her into their group.

As a result—they became a bandit trio.

When someone was after them, Sonia's warning shots got them out of most situations.

She didn't look like a gunslinger—at least not until someone saw her use them. She even managed to make good use of the recoil.

Pamela had acquired some entirely unexpected "muscle." She felt rather guilty about that, since Sonia didn't seem to really understand the situation. But that wasn't enough to stop her from pulling off jobs with the smooth-talking Lana. They were just the sort of small-time villains you could find in any big city, plus a useful, trigger-happy girl.

Now that they'd picked up an unexpected windfall, they thought they might be able to earn a little coin. Anyone who was making enough to live in a grand mansion like that during a recession like this one had to be involved in at least a little dirty business. In that case, it might be fun to take a bit of that money for themselves.

Based on that self-centered thought, these small-timers had put their kidnapping plan into action, but now…

⇔

The driver's seat of the jalopy

"Well, the plan's already gone south. Now what, Lana?"

"…It's not my fault."

They'd designated this bungalow as the site for the ransom handoff.

Their truck was parked in the light from the lamp near the bungalow's entrance.

In other words, the deserted bungalow they needed was now occupied.

Gazing at the two trucks that were parked in front of theirs, Pamela heaved a big sigh. "Right. It's my fault for letting you call them before we got a look at the handoff site. I'll apologize for that. I'm sorry."

"Huh...?"

Her partner was giving her a genuine apology, and Lana didn't know how to react. Flustered, she said the first thing that came into her head. "Th-that's nothing to worry about! I mean, if you apologize, I'll start thinking our situation's really hopeless!"

"As a matter of fact, it is."

"Stop that! Somebody just abandoned these trucks here! I'm telling you, there's nobody inside! Even if there is, they'll leave any minute now! I mean, you know... They've got trucks!"

"Quit talking applesauce. For now, let's get out and see."

Somber, Pamela opened her door, and Lana hastily prepared to get out as well. All she had to do was unfasten her seat belt and open the door, but Pamela's sincere apology had boggled her mind enough to slow her down a bit. Lana, Sonia, and Cazze ended up leaving the truck at almost the same time.

For the moment, they all gathered around Pamela and began to discuss what to do next. Cazze still had no idea that he'd been kidnapped, so Pamela and the others had to talk around that important bit of information.

As a matter of fact, Sonia hadn't been told about the kidnapping, either.

Considering the girl's personality, Lana worried Sonia was likely to tell Cazze about it or let him get away out of sympathy. Pamela had agreed. Neither of them disliked Sonia's tranquil personality, but she wasn't wired for kidnappings, and the experience would be unpleasant for her as well. So Pamela and Lana were the only ones really implementing the plan.

...*Come to think of it, this was pretty reckless.* It was a little late for that sort of thing, but privately, Pamela had started to feel regret.

Until a short while ago, they'd been gearing up for a train robbery. The recklessness of that plan by comparison had given her the illusion that kidnapping would be extremely practical.

Lana was still plenty eager to go ahead with it. On the way here, she'd gone so far as to say, "If we play our cards right, we'll be able to get both the ransom and the train passengers' money!" Pamela had smacked her upside the head and shut her up, but Lana wouldn't let go of the idea so quickly.

Although Pamela had thought kidnapping would be relatively easy, now they'd run into other people at the handoff site, which should have been deserted. She was regretting all her choices, and her nerves were starting to fray.

It isn't as if we can pick another handoff site now.

If the other party had already left the mansion with the money, they'd definitely miss them on the way. Unless both Cazze and their target were at the handoff, the target would probably report them to the police with no regard for appearances. Actually, it was best to assume they'd already done so.

That made it all the more important for the transaction to go off without a hitch.

In the worst-case scenario, if their plans went any further off course, they could leave Cazze here and make a run for it. If the other party showed up, no doubt they'd take the boy home, and while the trio wouldn't get the money, they'd be much more likely to make a clean getaway.

That was why Pamela had exited the truck in order to get a better picture of what they were dealing with.

Unfortunately, when she looked at the bungalow, she saw the face of the earlier visitor in the window.

Well, *visitors* in the plural, actually.

"……"

Having all those eyes staring at her through the window was incredibly disturbing. But Pamela hid it well as she looked away and spoke to Lana and Sonia. "…That's the place I was planning to use today. Apparently, someone beat us to it."

"Awww. What'll we dooo?" Sonia asked, although she didn't sound concerned.

Quietly, Pamela scanned the area nearby, then focused on the remaining huts.

"…For now, let's go look at the other bungalows."

⇔

His ears began to pick up another sound.

It was the engine of the bandit trio's worn-out truck.

Two other engines had passed by a little while earlier, but *he'd* still been dozing then. Now that *he* was gradually waking up, *he* caught the sound clearly. There was something nostalgic about it. A very similar noise had been his constant companion.

It was the sound of a vehicle that had carried him.

There was no telling what went through his mind when *he* heard that noise, but the thought made him sit up sluggishly.

Soon, the engine shut off, and the noise fell silent.

He swayed a little, then lay down on the floor again. With that big mound of food in front of him, *he* strained his ears again. *He* wouldn't let the tiniest sound from outside slip past him.

A memory rose in his half-awake brain.

Back when *he'd* been surrounded by human voices.

When countless sounds had been all around him.

When humans had approached him without fear.

In the end, it wasn't clear whether *he* had drawn any distinctions between humans and himself.

Had *he* accurately understood the difference? Humans couldn't tell. There was no way they could know.

Several images flashed into his mind from the ocean of his memory. Voices rang out. Sounds echoed. A multitude of different noises rained down over him. Yet his memories showed him more than that.

Someone who attracted more of those noises than *he* did.

The image of the one *he'd* had the most contact with—a man with blazing-red hair.

*　　*　　*

It might have been because *he'd* gotten to his feet earlier. The cycles of sleep and wakefulness began to grow shorter, and his blood started moving faster.

Quietly, *he* raised his head, then raised his voice.
He wanted to make his drowsy mind catch up with his waking body.
He just called out. That was all.

⇔

Bungalow Number 3

"OoooooOOoooOoOOOOooough…"

"Hmm?"
Just outside the door, Lana paused for a moment. She thought she'd heard a beast growl somewhere.
I wonder if they've got coyotes here.
She listened carefully for a little while but didn't hear anything else. Without giving it any further thought, she went inside.

"All right. Question of the hour: Should we stay in this bungalow tonight?" As Pamela spoke, she was looking around the interior of the barren hut.
She'd parked the truck in front of the bungalow, facing backward, as a theft deterrent. Now she was acquainting herself with the contents of the shed.
It held a single large table, iron hooks that were probably used to hang up captured prey, and wooden shelves. The hut wasn't even half the size of the first bungalow, but it was plenty big enough for four people—one of whom was a child—to spend half a day in.
"Are you okay? You're not cold, are you?" she asked Cazze.
Cazze was wearing a baggy winter coat they'd had in the back of

the truck. He peered up at her with innocent eyes, answering honestly, "No, miss, thank you very much!"

"O-oh, okay…" Pamela averted her eyes; his straightforward reply had landed a direct strike to her heart.

Drat. Maybe we really should have called this off.

Since he was the son of a rich man, she'd assumed he'd be a naïve, pampered boy, a spoiled little brat with aristocratic demands. In reality, this kid was very practical for his age, and he was ignorant of the world in a different way. He'd believed in them easily. He seemed oblivious to the possibility of bad people in the world, and his gaze was making her feel terribly guilty.

"Well, play with Sonia for a little while longer. Lana and I are going to go say hello to the people in the other bungalow."

"Okay!"

"We'll be back… Come on, let's go."

"Huh? Wait, I just got inside— Ow-ow-ow-ow, that hurts; you're hurting me!"

Pamela had begun feeling uncomfortable, and she pulled on Lana's arm, marching her outside. After they'd walked a short distance, she turned to her. "Listen, let's not do this after all."

"Wh-where did that come from?!"

"I'm not sure how to put it… Using a little kid like that is…you know…"

"What are you talking about?! It's no different from our robberies. Crimes are crimes! Why are you acting all goody-goody now?!" She scowled behind her glasses. Although her words were sharp, her eyes were clearly anxious and bewildered, and there was hesitation in them.

"…Well, maybe so, but not all crimes are created equal. Some people act like saints most of the time and still violate the Prohibition Act. Besides…"

"B-besides…what?"

"Even you aren't actually sure about this, are you, Lana?"

Instantly, Lana's face froze.

She started to argue, but Pamela got in first. "Why can't there be different types of villains, too? When we pull off robberies, maybe the person in charge of that casino or bank gets fired, or has a finger or two cut off, or gets rubbed out altogether. We say 'So what?' and keep knocking places over anyway. We're lowlifes. But even we hate the kind of lowlifes who'd lie to a kid right to his face, then take advantage of family ties to milk his folks for money. It all comes down to our personal preference. Right?"

"…Well, now you're being hypocritical. Just because the kid is right there… The person in charge of that casino might have a family, too; you're gonna ignore them? I never took you for a self-centered hypocrite, Pamela—" Lana couldn't seem to meet her eyes, and when she'd gotten that far, Pamela put her index finger against Lana's lips, silencing her. "Mrgle…"

Pamela leaned in close. There was a shrewd smile of amusement on her lips. "Aren't you forgetting something? Sonia's different, but both you and I are lowlifes. Bad guys, enemies of society at large. Remember?" That grin was still pasted on her lips, but the eyes she fixed on her friend had her usual twinkle in them. She spoke like a child revealing a prank.

"Of course villains are hypocrites. What else would we be?"

"……"

Lana gazed at her for a little while. Then she sighed, giving up. "Fine. I'll consider that proposal. That's all I'll do, though. Think about it."

"Thanks. But there's no telling how many years it'll take you to reach a conclusion, so don't brood too much."

"…I would've appreciated that comment more if it didn't have that middle bit…" Watching Pamela from beneath half-lowered lids, she went over her plan again, reluctant to part with it. "I really don't think we need to feel all that guilty, though… I mean, if they're living in a palace during a recession, you know they're doing something at least a little crooked to get their money."

"I thought so, too, but looking at that kid makes me think I might be wrong."

"Besides, when I demanded the ransom, I told them, 'Bring as much as you can of what you're able to pay.'"

"...If their kid hadn't actually gone missing, that condition would make anyone think this was a prank." Pamela pursed her lips.

Lana blushed a little, looking away. "Aw, geez. Don't compliment me like that."

"Uh, I'm not."

"Compliment me more directly, then!"

Are you stupid or something?! She almost screamed it at her, but before she could—

"Those glasses are the elephant's instep! I could tell you you're gorgeous a hundred times!"

The words had come from a young man who was standing right next to them.

""?!""

Pamela and Lana turned in unison. A boy dressed like a thug was there, all alone. He strode right up to Lana and clasped her hand firmly in both of his. "There, I complimented you! So please be my little sister, ma'am!"

"Wha—?! Um, huh?!" Lana was flustered.

Pamela cut in between them, her voice tense as she spoke to the boy. "W-wait a second. Who are you?! You just came out of nowhere— What do you want?"

"If you're asking me who I am... Yeah, I'm your big brother! As for what I'm after, I just want to make you two my little sisters. That's all!"

"What in... Wh-what? You're talking bunkum; what do you mean?!"

I seriously don't understand what he's saying, but..., Pamela thought.

Did he...hear us?! Lana thought. Both were in a panic.

If this kid had in fact overheard them, it wouldn't be a question of whether to carry out the kidnapping anymore. They'd have to choose whether to cut and run, silence this boy, or cover for themselves somehow.

"Sh-she's right! Just telling us to be your little sisters out of the blue… A girl's got to prepare herself for these things!"

"You be quiet, Lana." Shutting up her partner before she could make things worse, Pamela turned back toward the boy—and then she noticed something alarming.

Huh?

The kid who was yelling about little sisters wasn't the only one there.

From behind the truck, silently, truly without a sound—

—the group of girls and boys who'd been in the first bungalow a moment earlier were watching them.

?! ! ?! ? ? ?!

She couldn't have been more confused.

The darkness had probably helped, but a group this big had crept up behind them without making any noise. She shuddered.

"EEeeeEEEeep?!" Lana had also registered the "throng" of gazes. With a wild shriek, she ducked behind Pamela.

"Are you, um…the kids who are using the bungalow next door? Are you camping out here?" Operating on a faint hope, she tried to muddy the waters with a question, but—

—a girl with sleepy eyes and watches on both arms gave a languid smile, then struck Pamela and Lana with despair as she said: "No, we were just killing time. It's nice to meet you, *kidnappers.*"

Savoring both anticipation and happiness, like a child who'd found a favorite toy, she cheerfully smiled, and smiled, and smiled.

"So can you give us the lowdown on what you were discussing forty-seven seconds ago?!"

⟺

Meanwhile   In the woods

"Comrade Sarges. We've uncovered something concerning."

"What?"

"The negotiators have found a potential obstacle."

"Just a minute."

A wide river cut through the forest.

A long bridge bisected that river.

The tracks of the transcontinental railway ran over that bridge, and a local train was currently crossing them, spewing noise and soot.

Having made their camp in the woods not too far from that bridge, the men in military uniforms were conversing calmly. Sarges made sure the train had completed its crossing, then turned to his subordinate. "Let's hear it. What is this 'potential obstacle'?"

Although they wore military uniforms, it was likely that even someone who was well versed in such matters wouldn't have been able to tell what unit, or even which army, they belonged to. Their uniforms were the only ones of their kind in the world. Paired with their design, it made the group seem like the ghosts of a ruined country.

"The young people we saw in the forest earlier have relocated to the bungalows at Point K."

"...Point K?" The name made Sarges grimace. "Are you sure?"

"Yes, sir. The two trucks we saw were parked there, and one bungalow's lights were on."

"There, of all places..." The man *tsk*ed.

"The negotiators will pass that point on their way back," his subordinate reminded him, although his face was still calm. "They may be seen."

"Can we contact the negotiators?"

"Not immediately. Our wireless is out of range."

They were members of the Lemures, a terrorist group run by Huey Laforet. While another unit was occupying the Flying Pussyfoot, their job was to negotiate with the government, using the train's passengers as hostages.

There was only a little time left before the train's occupation was scheduled to begin.

The five who were directly in charge of the negotiations were supposed to return to this camp at fixed intervals during the operation, one at a time, to deliver status reports.

They'd plotted a route that would prevent the police from following them, and that route went right past the bungalows.

If they were going to be absolutely sure, they needed to eliminate any risk that they might be spotted, but—

"With numbers like that, even liquidating them wouldn't be a sure thing." Sarges said *liquidate* as if it meant nothing to him, then went on impassively. "Let's send two scouts. If they seem unlikely to cause trouble, don't disturb them. If they do pose a problem, they're obstacles. Get rid of them. Don't use guns if you can help it."

Choosing two men who were nearby, he sent them off toward the bungalow.

From the shadows, Sarges watched his subordinates go. "All right… Eight hours remaining until the appointed time."

He spoke to himself—and in the darkness, where no one could see him, he smiled quietly.

"Let's give Senator Beriam an opportunity to demonstrate his character and skills."

Chapter 4   Bunny Hasty & Bunny Tasty

"If they're living in a palace during a recession, you know they're doing something at least a little crooked to get their money."

Pamela's thoughts on Cazze's family weren't entirely the self-centered delusion of a two-bit villain.

She'd gotten one thing very wrong, though: *a little* didn't begin to cover it.

The Runorata Family had amassed its fortune by doing "crooked things" openly, on a massive scale. That was the truth.

They were one of the largest, most powerful syndicates on the East Coast. Their greatest asset wasn't money or muscle, but an individual named Bartolo Runorata.

Some of the organization's most brilliantly insane individuals were there to protect him. They were Bartolo's personal guards, a group that got ahead in a different way from the executives.

They weren't expected to repel active attackers. The only thing anyone cared about was how effectively they could take a bullet for their boss.

They were members of the Runorata Family who didn't want success and had no interest in climbing the ladder. They simply idolized Bartolo. Instead of squandering their lives, they were capable of throwing them away rationally, at the best possible time.

Bartolo's personal guard was made up of people like these.

Because he understood this, he placed the utmost trust in them—and used them up completely.

He knew that, as far as they were concerned, this was the greatest compliment he could pay them.

Although being able to take a bullet for their boss was the biggest requirement, that didn't mean they had no other skills. Some of them could double as outstanding assault troops or assassins.

The twins who were riding through the night on motorbikes were two of these shields who could fight back.

Late night   Upstate New York   Near the forest

"Well now, what should we do, I?"

"Good question, Me."

Straddling identical bikes, the peculiar young men were calling each other I and Me.

They'd stopped in the woods along the road that led to the designated bungalow and were lying low. The conversation between them didn't mean much.

"We're almost at the handoff site, I."

"It's just up this road, Me."

"Shall we go?"

"Let's watch and wait a little longer, Me. If we rush it and they take the young master hostage, we'll have even more trouble to deal with."

Although the subject they were discussing was tense—they were smiling.

"By the way, I, how much cash do I have?"

"Oh, right. Hang on a sec, Me."

After exchanging looks, they both checked the contents of their wallets.

"Just looked, Me. There's twenty bucks, tops."

"Indeed, I. This wallet has a whole twelve dollars even."

"So that's thirty-two bucks between the two of us, huh?"

"That's a problem."

Sighing, the two shook their heads in unison.

"What did the criminal demand?"

"They said to give as much as we could."

"Will they settle for thirty-two dollars?"

"They'd better."

The two chuckled quietly together. Gradually, an unpleasant light came into their eyes.

"And if they don't?"

"Then we go on the hunt."

"What will we do if something happens to the young master, I?"

"Well, obviously, we'll kill 'em all."

Get Cazze back. That is all. What should you do with the kidnappers? I don't care. That's up to you.

Those were their orders from their great and beloved boss.

Ordinarily, their only opportunity to show their loyalty would have been to take a bullet for him and die—but now they'd been assigned a mission besides security work.

They'd originally been something like button men for the syndicate, but due to their recklessness, they'd been pulled from the front lines for targeting people they didn't have to.

Guarding the boss had been their pride and joy. However, now that they'd received another order, delight of a different kind was welling up inside them.

They were dyed-in-the-wool battle addicts, and they'd been waiting eagerly for a chance to make the most of the skills they'd cultivated.

At the same time, they were also angry.

They wanted to strike back at the arrogant kidnappers who'd had the nerve to snatch Cazze, the future of their beloved Family.

Experiencing this anger and delight simultaneously, they quietly scanned their surroundings.

They traveled slowly through the deep forest, staying back far enough that they couldn't be seen from the road. Then, suddenly, they heard an engine.

A few seconds later, a truck raced down the road, past the forest where they were hiding. Its tires had been designed for off-road use, and the man in the driver's seat wore a strange military uniform that wasn't from any country they knew.

When they saw his clothes, the twins looked at each other, then nodded.

At the exact same moment, they gunned their bikes' engines and burst out onto the road, chasing the truck.

⟺

The member of the Lemures headed back to the camp was beyond rattled.

He'd been sure the cops weren't tailing him. Even if he had somehow picked up a shadow, he'd been confident that he'd lost it completely.

…So who were these two bikers who'd appeared out of nowhere?

They couldn't just be kids on a joyride, or they wouldn't have come out of the woods.

The bikes looked like military models, and they were clearly following him on purpose.

The man had no idea what was happening. His mind went to the equipment on the passenger seat. *What do I do? I can't let them follow me back to the base. Even if we all tried to get rid of them, if they got away, we'd be done for.*

Should I get rid of them at the bungalows at Point K?

Just as his thoughts turned to the huts that lay up ahead, he caught a glimpse of something strange out of the corner of his eye. In the rearview mirror, the two bikes got so close they seemed to overlap, then fused into one.

"—?!"

Hastily, he focused on the rearview mirror, but there really was only one bike reflected in it.

"That's insane!!" Without thinking, he cried out, and as he looked around, he realized something.

The bikes' apparent fusion had been an optical illusion, generated on purpose.

One bike was running parallel with the truck, its headlight extinguished—and its rider had taken advantage of his confusion to get a good look at him and the vehicle's interior.

Without hesitating, the man grabbed the handgun from the passenger seat, opened the window, and fired.

However—the bike actually pulled closer to the truck. Neatly slipping past the bullet, the rider put out a hand. "Bingo! We knew you weren't just a kidnapper!"

A kidnapper?! What is he talking abababababaaaaaaaaaaaaaa aaaaaaah!

"DaaAAaaaGaaaah!"

The driver was screaming before he could even ask the question.

The biker had caught the wrist of his gun hand and violently twisted it up.

"Agaaah! Ah, gah, whaaaa?! GaaaAAAaah!"

The first scream was one of pain.

"Aaaah! ...AAAAaaaaWAAaah!"

The one that followed it was of fear.

His hands had left the wheel completely for a few seconds, and now the trees were right in his face.

The crash echoed loudly through the silence that dominated the night.

$$\Longleftrightarrow$$

Ten minutes later   Near Bungalow Number 7

"...He's late."

"Yes, he really should have been passing us right about now."

The Lemures who'd been ordered to scout out the bungalows exchanged dubious looks.

Despite the winter cold, the pair had been observing Bungalow

Number 1, which had been noisy the entire time. However, the negotiator's failure to appear was making them uneasy for reasons that had nothing to do with the bungalow.

They'd been watching from the shadows of Number 7 for several hours now, but the boys and girls inside hadn't done anything that seemed to warrant much caution.

The fact that there was a third truck now concerned them, but the only bungalows with lights on were 1 and 3. The rest were still vacant.

They should probably assume that a group of young people had swarmed in and was camping in the bungalows without permission.

If the negotiation team simply drove by, there wouldn't be a problem.

…Or so they'd thought, but the negotiator hadn't shown up.

"…Did something happen?"

"What should we do? Should we report in to Comrade Sarges?"

They were conversing urgently. Meanwhile, the contrasting clamor from Bungalow Number 1 grew even louder, until the raucous voices reached all the way to their hiding spot.

"Dammit… Easygoing bunch, aren't they," one of the Lemures spat.

But there was something they hadn't noticed.

As the voices grew louder, *he* was almost fully awake in Bungalow Number 7.

Then a few minutes later:

"…Something has to be wrong. I'll go back for now; you stay here."

"Right."

The first man turned back to the wall of Number 7…

Creak…

…and registered a soft sound.

The door was swinging slightly in the breeze.

Huh…? I'm pretty sure that was closed…just a minute ago.

When they'd first arrived, they'd looked in through the windows, but all they'd seen was darkness.

Their first and greatest mistake had been not actually going inside to check. They'd avoided it because they hadn't wanted the group in the bungalow to hear the door open and close.

And even if they had gone in, it was *very likely* that the tragedy would only have happened sooner.

What...? What's that smell?

A faint, pungent odor they hadn't noticed before hung in the air.

Was something inside Bungalow Number 7?

A sudden tension ran through him, and he turned back to his companion.

The other man seemed to have noticed the smell, too; he frowned, confused. "...What stinks?"

"That's what I want to know. Maybe some travel rations went bad in there?"

Trying to guess at the source of the odor, they thought about what they'd seen when they looked in the window.

There hadn't been anything inside.

All they remembered was pitch-black darkness.

Unfortunately, they were wrong.

When they'd peeked into the room, they'd mistaken *him* for a pile of blankets.

If they'd strained their eyes or shone their lights in carefully, they would have noticed that the texture was wrong for blankets and that it was *moving* slightly.

He was enormous, though, and they'd only been able to see him as a mound of blankets.

They hadn't registered the massive amount of food piled up behind him, either—

—and as a result, they'd allowed *him* to get this close.

"That smell... I think it's getting stronger."

"No, this...is different from the other one..."

By the time they realized it was the smell of an animal, it was too late.

He had already left Bungalow Number 7—and was watching the Lemures from the brush right next to them.

The two uniformed men gulped, then quietly looked around the area.

They tried anyway.

But they didn't see him.

He was so big that, for a moment, their brains couldn't register him as a living creature.

However, that illusion didn't last long.

"...Hmm?"

"...Huh?"

Realizing that something was off, the two looked toward the brush on reflex.

This time, they saw it.

In the brush, something *inhuman* had risen to its feet.

Even when they realized what it was, the two of them couldn't will themselves to move.

It can't be.

That should never have been in a place like this. That common knowledge threw off their decision-making abilities.

That said, although they were low-ranking members, they were still Lemures.

They stayed frozen for only two seconds.

However—with that horrifying sight in front of them, those two seconds were fatal.

And so *his* time arrived.

An *enormous* grizzly bear who stood over nine feet tall, *he* threw his massive body at the two men in military uniforms.

The men's screams ripped through the night, drowning out the clamor from Bungalow Number 1.

That signaled the start of the great, crazy ruckus in the woods.

Digression

There was an as-yet-unaccounted-for gap in the life of Claire Stanfield.

Between his boyhood with Firo Prochainezo and his fame as Vino the hitman, there was a gap of about five years.

Firo knew he'd been scouted by a traveling circus and joined up after the Gandors' father had died. He wasn't familiar with the details, though. The next thing he knew, Claire had been a hitman.

However, that was only from Firo's perspective; of course Claire knew best what had happened in that time.

1927   New York

"So why'd you become a conductor anyway?"

Firo wasn't a Martillo Family executive yet. He was talking to his childhood pal, who was back home on a visit for the first time in ages.

The young redhead, Claire Stanfield, was using a fork to fiddle with the plate of spaghetti in front of him. "Well, I'm a hitman and all. Free travel all over the States is pretty convenient."

"That's it?"

"That's it...or I wish I could say it was anyway. This cook who kept us fed back when I was in the circus has been working his way around the dining cars of those fancy, expensive trains. He put in a good word for me."

The circus. When he heard Claire mention his former occupation, Firo broached the topic somewhat hesitantly. "So, uh…I hear the circus broke up."

Claire didn't seem too down about it as he answered absently. "Sure did. Although the ringmaster did say he'd start it up again once things calm down. Right now I'm a hitman and conductor, so I'll be focusing on that for a while."

"Once what calms down?"

"Eh, we got into some trouble with a pretty big gang, and the troupe scattered. By the time the ringmaster and I put 'em down, there were almost no carnies left."

"Uh, you know that's incredible, right? You said it like it was nothing." Firo broke out in a cold sweat.

"Did I? There wasn't anything incredible about it. What was incredible was our troupe. The magician fella? Amazing. He wore these clothes that sparkled like jewel beetles, but he called himself a vampire. His tricks really were fantastic, though. He produced bats from his hand instead of doves, and he walked around after he'd been cut in two."

"You…you sure those were tricks?"

"There were plenty of other types, too. The cook would twist up manhole covers, and there were these acrobats who'd have kung fu battles up on the trapeze. I used to join in, but I always won, so they shut me out."

Closing his eyes as he remembered the past, Claire nodded. "Our star girl's show was great. She had this cute little face, and she'd put on boxing gloves; for a dollar, anybody in the audience could go a round with her. If they won, they'd get a hundred bucks. Mostly time ran out before they managed to land a punch; sometimes they'd be slimeballs who just wanted to punch a girl or constantly clinched her on purpose. Those guys, she KO'd. I tell you what, she was tough."

"I'm not sure your group was actually a circus." Firo was still sweating.

"In the end, I'm the only one who managed to get that hundred bucks," Claire told him.

"What, you took her on?!" Firo gave his friend an accusing glare.

Claire quickly defended himself, visibly upset. "Hey, whoa, don't write me off for that. I didn't hit any girls. I stopped right before I made contact, like you're supposed to, and made her admit I won. I also told her, 'If you want me to return this hundred, go on a date with me.'"

"……"

"…Right after that, she clocked me right on the chin, and I took that as a no."

"Too bad she didn't hit you a hundred more times," Firo retorted, exasperated by his friend's wild ways. "You're unbelievable. How can you just walk up and tell a girl your feelings?"

It was a perfectly natural complaint, but Claire grinned. "Because this world is mine. Someday, the girl who's best for me is going to tell me yes, and the timing's gonna be perfect."

"Where do you get that self-confidence?"

"Hey, it's not just about my girl. Everyone I meet is a character in the world that is 'me.' If I need them, I know I'll see them again. If I don't, then I didn't need 'em that bad." Claire sounded delusional, but that was nothing new. Firo only shook his head. "That being the case, I'm not too torn up about it. The fact that the circus broke up, I mean. Someday, when the right time comes around, I'll probably see the ringmaster and the other fellas and Cookie again."

"Cookie?" Firo asked. The word had come out of nowhere. "What's that? Did the circus sell branded cookies or something?"

"No, no. Huh? Didn't I tell you about Cookie?"

"Nope, not a thing."

"I see… Maybe it was Keith and the other guys I told, then." Claire scratched his cheek.

"Cookie was my rival for top star at the circus…"

Interlude

"Your name's Cookie. Yeah, that's it."

There was no telling how the hairy creature had taken the red-headed boy's remark; in the next instant, without so much as a growl, it sank its fangs into the kid.

1920s   In a circus tent somewhere in America

A moment later, the grizzly bear who'd been dubbed "Cookie" froze.

Ordinarily, he would have torn the flesh away and the bone with it, then used his claws and fangs to shove his opponent to the ground.

Instead, Cookie stiffened.

His teeth, which could easily bite through a tree, didn't sink any deeper into the boy's arm.

A moment later, Cookie's jaws sprang open as fast as they'd snapped closed, and he rolled on the ground, flapping his arms, almost as if his upper half had been burned.

When they saw that, the people standing outside the cage shouted and whooped.

The whole group was patently odd: There was someone dressed in European armor, and a muscular man who was built like a ball, and another who was as tall and thin as a wire, and another who wore Japanese-style armor.

That said, in a circus tent, none of them looked terribly out of place.

"Nee-hee-hee, what's the matter? What happened, Claire? Hee-hee-hee," asked a clown who was laughing behind a "sad face" mask.

"Oh, I slathered my arm in Tabasco sauce," Claire answered casually.

"He bit you real good, though, didn't he? Didn't he bite you just now?" asked a girl in a spiderweb leotard; she sounded worried.

Claire smiled at her. "Yeah, but it'll heal right up. A little deeper, and he would've broken the bone."

The boy was talking as if he'd been bitten by a dog, and a young man who'd been watching from a distance burst out laughing. "Ah-ha-ha-ha-ha! You win that bet, Claire!"

The guy's right eye had been badly wounded, and the socket held a red crystal instead of his eyeball.

Chuckling as if it was nothing, Claire reminded his employer: "You promised, Ringmaster! No getting rid of Cookie!"

"All right, all right. I won't turn him into bear stew. Well, you don't want that getting infected. Go get some cooking sherry from Mr. Gregoire and pour it on there!"

"Yessir!" the kid said energetically, and the surrounding circus folk cheered.

"That was really somethin'! You actually let him bite your right arm."

"And he didn't tear it off... What kind of muscles have you got in there, huh? Hee-hee!"

"That's incredible! Geniuses come off looking slick no matter what they do!"

In response to the compliments, the boy just sighed and shook his head. "I keep telling you, I'm no genius. I work hard for this."

At that, the ringmaster grinned. "For you, hard work can accomplish *anything*. That's a mighty fine talent, Claire."

*　　*　　*

Whether that conversation had reached him or not, *he* felt the burning in his mouth finally ease.

Even among grizzlies, *he* was a bit unique.

Maybe *he'd* eaten well; *he'd* been growing bigger than most of his kind when, one day, humans had captured him. Just when they were about to kill him, a circus troupe had picked him up. Caged as an enormous beast, *he'd* grown more savage by the day, until *he'd* even tried to attack his trainer.

At that point, the redheaded newbie had said "I'll settle him down" and marched into his cage. The rest of the troupe hadn't stopped him, which meant they were definitely crazy, too. In the end, the kid had survived, and *he'd* ended up rolling around the giant cage.

He didn't understand any of these human circumstances, though.

From that day on, *he* started to behave for his trainer.

He knew: If *he* obeyed the instructions the trainer and the boy gave him, and the big crowds of humans cheered, his daily meals would get bigger and better.

Over the next several months, "Cookie" came to understand three things clearly...even if some of them weren't entirely correct.

First: When people cheered, it was a good thing as far as his own survival was concerned.

Second: The creatures known as "humans" were poisonous to eat.

Third: The redhead who hadn't struck back after being bitten was his pal.

After that, *he* spent several years with the boy, the circus troupe, and the lion, tiger, anaconda, and other animals that were in the cages next to his. Cookie was satisfied with that state of affairs. At some point, meals stopped being part of the equation for him, and the mere sound of the audience's cheers began to make him feel something like happiness.

After another several years...

When the circus broke up, the beast tamer had taken Cookie all around America. At least until they were eventually separated.

As a result, *he'd* ended up wandering the woods of upstate New York, all by himself.

It wasn't clear what was going through his mind, but *he* hadn't let any humans notice his presence.

He just kept on wandering through the forest.

Chapter 5　　　Run like a Bunny

Bungalow Number 1

While the giant beast was lunging at the two Lemures, the mood in the bungalow couldn't have been less tense.

"Nwuh? I just heard…a scream or something."
"Yeah? I bet it was your imagination."
"Hya-haah!" "Hya-haaaw."
The room should have seemed spacious, but it was currently swarming with kids of all different ages.
"Forget that—how much longer until we hit the road?"
"Ask Melody."
"Don't you want to take it easy for another three days or so?"
"The cargo will all wash downriver."
"We can just go to the coast and pick it up."
"Don't talk crazy."
"The coast, huh…? I want to see the dolls swimming in their birthday suits."
"Man, I can't believe you just said that out loud."
"I want to see 'em, too, though." "Me too." "And me." "Me three!" "So do I!"
"You're a doll yourself!" "Hey, some girls want to see girls naked sometimes!"

"What...?!" "Why'd you go and make it sexy?!"

"Okay, fine! Be my little sister." "That made no sense!"

"Hya-haah!" "Hya-haw." "Gyaaaah-ha-ha-ha-ha-ha!"

Swarming really was the word for it: They were milling about like confused ants.

In the midst of that bizarre conversation, a few figures stood out sharply from the crowd.

Pamela and Lana were in a corner, watching the noisy group of kids. Sonia was sleeping peacefully beside them while the delinquent girls were treating Cazze like a dress-up doll.

"P-p-please stop."

They were changing him into and out of girls' clothes, and his face was bright red. But the girls squealed with laughter and kept right on dressing him up.

As they watched the lighthearted chaos, Pamela and Lana exchanged looks, then began conversing in whispers.

"...What should we do, Pamela?"

"There's nothing to do, period. Whatever's going to happen will happen."

"But that's leaving everything to chance!"

"I never thought I'd be hearing that from you, Lana... Well, it's good as far as you're concerned, isn't it? It means we'll be pulling that train job after all." Pamela smiled wryly.

Lana heaved a big sigh. "Do coincidences like this even happen? Who'd have believed we'd come to rob a train and run into train robbers..."

"Obviously, they do. Did you forget about the museum incident?" Pamela said dryly. Lana sighed again.

On the train they were targeting, the web of coincidences and sheer lunacy made this seem normal by comparison—but they had no way of knowing that. Instead, they remembered the exchange they'd had a little while earlier.

⇔

A few hours previously

"So how much are you ladies planning to bleed that rich family for?" The question had come from a girl with pigtails, sleepy eyes, and a silly smile.

Lana averted her gaze, breaking out in a cold sweat. "Wh-what are you talking about? We aren't really..."

"You don't have to hide it. Thirty-four seconds ago, you said, 'Besides, when I demanded the ransom, I told them, "Bring as much as you can of what you're able to pay."'" Giggling, the girl repeated Lana's earlier remark with the precision of a tape recorder.

"Seriously, who are you?" Going pale, Lana turned to the side and grasped for a way out. "That's right! You can't prove I said anything of the sort! Heh-heh-heh-heh. It's an amusing deduction, but it sounds like you should be writing mysteries instead."

Lana was suddenly bursting with confidence. Sighing heavily, Pamela looked down—and the kids around them began energetically objecting.

"Nah, I heard her, too." "And me." "Me too." "Be my little sister." "Me too." "Me too." "Marry me."

"And actually, uh...that wasn't a deduction so much as an eyewitness account."

"Yeah, nothing to do with writers."

"Is this lady stupid?"

"Hey, dumbbell! If you call somebody stupid, you're stupid! Be more subtle about it!"

"Good point. Then, uh... Oh. Excuse me, miss? Is there something wrong with you somewhere, physically? Especially, uh, behind your eyeballs, inside your skull?" the boy asked politely.

Lana whispered in Pamela's ear. "Um... Is my color that bad?"

"No, but your brain is."

"That's mean! How could you say that, Pamela?!" Lana protested with a shocked look.

Pushing the other woman's head out of the way, Pamela turned to the boys with a sigh of defeat. "Kids, this girl wears glasses, but she's not too bright. You can't expect subtle insults to work on her." With a smile that didn't go past her lips, Pamela gave the group a quiet once-over—then spoke a bit defiantly. "Well, what are you going to do? Send us to the cops? Blackmail us? Just so you know, the kidnappee hasn't figured it out yet, and I don't want to scare him if I can help it."

She seemed to be pushing her luck, but the boys looked at one another, then started to talk it over among themselves.

"What do we do?"

"Well, obviously... What, you haven't come up with anything?!"

"Hya-haah!"

"Shaddap! Chaini, say something besides 'Hya-haah,' wouldja?!"

"The humane thing would probably be to rescue the child. However, since we're helping out with a train robbery, we aren't really qualified to throw stones."

"Don't get serious out of nowhere! No one knows how to react!"

"Hya-haw!"

"Close your head, Parrot! You gotta say something besides 'Hya-haw,' too!"

".........Die."

"Did you just say 'Die'?! Was that little whisper 'Die'?!"

"Hya-haw!"

"I—I guess I was hearing stuff."

Meanwhile, the girl with pigtails took a step toward Pamela and leaned in close. She seemed to be enjoying herself. "What do you want us to do, ladies?"

"Huh?!" Pamela was bewildered.

The girl gave her a quiet smile. "All I care about is killing time constructively until the train robbery. So...I don't mind going along with your plan until then."

Had this been a lucky miscalculation as far as Pamela's group was concerned?

The kids who'd overheard their plan weren't utter villains, but they certainly weren't the good guys, either.

And then—Pamela and Lana learned something else.

This gang of delinquents was planning to do what their trio had originally intended: steal the Flying Pussyfoot's cargo.

⇔

"They say they've already got people on the train. It does sound hit-or-miss, but they're being a lot more systematic than we were."

"Hmph! I don't know about that. I mean, I hope they manage to make it to the freight car. It's their first time on that train; they won't know left from right. In that case, the plan I came up with is…"

As Lana muttered, one of the delinquents slung an arm around her shoulders. "It's fine; they're part of the train crew. We've got two pals on the staff."

The boy leaned against her, being overly friendly. Lana pried him off. "On the staff…?"

"Well, the cook and bartender on that train have been tight with us for ages! They gave us the wire about the cargo and stuff!" the kid said proudly.

Pamela sounded a little appalled. "Are you sure it's all right to tell us that?"

"? Why not?"

"If we get picked up by the cops, don't you think we might squeal on your group while we're there?"

This was a perfectly natural question, but the boy seemed mystified. "Well, don't get caught, then."

"……"

Pamela couldn't find a response for a little while.

During that moment of silence, the boys and girls crowded around them.

"Boy, are you dumb. Who knows whether they're gonna get caught?"

"They could turn themselves in, too."

"Huh?! Why?! Are you ladies gonna turn yourselves in?!" The boy sounded flustered.

Lana responded with complete confidence. "Of course we won't!

Our dream is to become the best gang of bandits in America! We won't turn ourselves in, and we won't let the cops collar us!"

The kids all shouted over one another.

"Oooooooh!"

"I don't really get it, but that sounded awesome!"

"I'd expect no less…of my little sister!" "Shove it." "My big sister, then!" "Well, okay." "Wait, it is?!"

"How do they figure out who's the best bandit?"

"Well, come on, by… Uh, by how much they stole, maybe…"

"They'd tally it all up?!"

"By instinct, then!"

"Instinct, huh?!" "Yeah, that's real important for bandits!" "You're real smart." "Hya-haah!"

"I see… So bandits decide who's number one by instinct, huh?" "That's bandits for you." "Hya-haw!"

"By the way, if you're the best, do you get something?"

"I bet…somebody pays some kind of cash prize."

"They do?" "I bet not."

"Then just go steal it yourselves, huh?!"

"Whoa, why'd you get so mad?" "You make no sense."

"Well, it's fine! If that's all you ladies want!"

"Hya-haah!" "Hya-haw." "Gweh-heh-heh."

The chaotic mass of words echoed between Pamela and Lana.

I'm having trouble following all this, Pamela thought.

Yep, this is making no sense, Lana thought.

Pamela gave a sigh of exhaustion, then looked around.

Melody and the others were still messing with Cazze on the opposite side of the room. He seemed shy, but he was smiling; not a soul had told him he'd been kidnapped yet.

Meanwhile, over on this side…

"I really do think the three of us should have matching outfits. We have to get our name out there, you know!"

"…What about going stark naked?!"

"Stark naked?! Oh… That might be novel!" Lana was blending right in with the dim-witted conversation.

I don't exactly fit in here, but...
...this sort of thing is...kinda nice.
On that thought, Pamela gazed up at the ceiling for a while.

In the end, these boys and girls had found out about their plan.

Then, for some reason, the other group had also started telling them about their train robbery.

At first, Pamela hadn't been able to fathom why they'd do a thing like that, but as she listened to them talk, she'd begun to understand, in a way.

No, there was no way she could understand.

After all, they weren't thinking, period.

They were just living life as their instincts dictated.

As she watched them, something abruptly occurred to her.

So deep down, they're like us?

Reflecting on their past—and their uncertain future—she smiled wryly to herself.

Honestly. In other words, the only one in this entire group with a stable future is...Cazze.

But there was something she hadn't picked up on: the possibility that this boy they'd kidnapped might have the stormiest future of all.

It might not even be the distant future.

Pamela completely failed to anticipate the rough seas waiting just up ahead.

⟺

Deep in the forest   Near the iron bridge

An army truck and several private cars were stopped beside a tent pitched a short distance from the railroad tracks. At first glance, the cars looked normal. However, the license plates had all been forged.

Sarges and the other Lemures weren't indulging in small talk. Their method of killing time was the exact opposite of the one Melody's group had opted for.

"…They're late," Sarges muttered, glancing at his watch. It was significantly past the time the first negotiator had been scheduled to return. Not only that, but the men who'd been sent to observe those concerning delinquents were also nowhere to be seen.

"…What is this?"

The ordinary thing to assume was that there had been some sort of trouble, but he couldn't bring himself to believe that. When he'd seen the group in the woods earlier, they'd seemed like nothing more than a bunch of ne'er-do-wells. Naturally, he didn't believe they had any special training or that the two scouts had blundered.

"Unlikely" doesn't mean "impossible," however.

Some new complication might have appeared. For example, some third party could have joined them.

Sarges thought for a while. Then, checking his watch again, he issued orders.

"…All right. Two of you wait here," he said.

"The rest of you, come with me to Point K."

⇔

Near the forest's entrance

"Now then, what should we do about this, I?"

"Great question, Me."

The twin hunters were standing with folded arms, wearing brutal smiles. They were looking at a vehicle with a crumpled bumper and hood.

Although it wasn't in flames, it was clear that it wouldn't function as a vehicle anymore. There was a body hanging from a nearby tree. It had been strung up with a sturdy rope, and it was breathing faintly.

The person hadn't "survived" so much as been kept alive, just barely.

"The moment we said we wanted him to release the child, his expression changed."

"Yeah, he screamed 'Government dogs!' or something."

"To think he'd treat us, of all people, as government dogs."

It wasn't clear what the joke was, but the twins grinned at each other.

They'd dragged the "kidnapper" out of his truck and done a little interrogating. They'd failed to establish a discussion, though, and the man had ended up calling them government dogs until he passed out.

That said, while they hadn't learned whether Cazze was safe or not, they'd managed to threaten the man into telling them where he'd been headed.

"Through the bungalows up ahead, beside the railway bridge…"

"Is that where the young master is? Huh, Me?"

"We can only hope, I."

Sighing, the twins took another look at the man who was hanging behind them. Although he was unconscious now, he'd held up under their torture fairly well.

"Still… One does wonder why he called us government dogs."

"Maybe 'cause the boss is tight with Senator Beriam?"

The moment the suggestion was made, the young men's attitudes began to grow colder and colder.

"That means…these people think our Don Bartolo is lower than Senator Beriam. An idea as terrible as it is false. Is that it?"

"They're making monkeys of us, Me."

"Let's teach them a lesson, I."

The pair rolled their necks at the exact same time, cracking their joints rhythmically, and straddled their motorbikes.

Then, quietly, they rode away.

They were headed deeper into the forest, toward the cluster of bungalows, where a variety of "others" waited.

And so the visitors to the forest drew closer and closer.

*　　*　　*

The deep woods absorbed both malice and goodwill in equal measure, creating a unique space.

At this moment, at least…

…practically no one in it could be labeled a "good person."

⇔

Bungalow Number 1

"Nyup."

Sonia slowly sat up in a corner of the room, like a mollusk that had acquired human vocal cords. "Good mooorning, Pamela, Lana, and, ummm, crowd."

"There's not much point in calling them that."

The girl had slept soundly, completely unaffected by the surrounding situation. Putting on the helmet she'd set down by her chest, she smiled brightly with a long yawn. "Well, so what happened? Are Cazze's parents coming to pick him up?" she asked innocently. She still hadn't been told a thing about the kidnapping.

Lana and Pamela wore rather stiff smiles as they tried to gloss over the matter.

"Um, I think they could get here any minute, really…"

"N-never mind that— Are you sure you don't need to *maintain* and *test-fire* your guns today?"

"Wha—?! Lana!"

"Huh? Did I say something wrong?" Lana had already forgotten what she said, her eyes darting around behind her spectacles.

Before the kids around them could react to that remark, Pamela tried to shout something to distract them, but Sonia spoke first, in a chipper mood as always upon waking up. She didn't hesitate, and her smile was genuine.

"Oh, right! I need to do maintenance on about ten of them!"

*　　*　　*

A few minutes later

Most of the people who'd been in the bungalow were gathered around the bed of the jalopy.

Looking rather resigned, Pamela opened the canvas back. Lana was huddled at a distance, deep in self-loathing. In sharp contrast to the two of them, Sonia was happily watching Pamela work, and the rest were observing all three of them with deep interest.

"Just so you know, these are mementos of Sonia's family, so you mustn't steal them or fire them without permission," Pamela warned them.

The delinquents thumped their chests.

"We know that!"

"Trust us a little, wouldja?"

"…When they just met us?"

"No, actually, they can trust us *because* they just met us. The more time you spend with somebody, the more you get to see who they are, deep down, and the harder it is to trust 'em. Now, when we just met, they can trust us on pure instinct. Go on—put blind faith in us! You can even love us— Blughk!"

"Can it, perv!" "You heard him! Try to seduce my little sisters, will you!" "Die!" "'Die' was going too far!" "Okay then, suffer!" "Feel pain!" "Get hurt!" "I'll fry you!" "With the fires of hell!"

"Yaaaaaaaaaaaaaaaaaaaaugh!" "Hya-haah!" Gyah-haaah!"

The boy was getting pummeled in a way generally reserved for comedy films, but Pamela ignored him, silently unloading cargo from the bed of the truck.

Still, what are we going to do about Cazze? Will he accept that these are how Sonia remembers her parents?

Cazze hadn't caught on to the kidnapping yet, but wouldn't he get frightened if he saw guns?

Worried, she turned to him and wondered what she could say to distract him, but Cazze's expression hadn't changed a bit. He was watching her with a little smile.

Sonia had already started to take guns out of the crate, but he was unaffected.

Even the delinquents were saying things like "Whoa, are those real?!"

"Woooow. Compared with these, the ones we left back in Chicago were popguns."

"Yeah, the machine gun Jacuzzi used was the scariest one we had."

"Can you shoot a gun this long with those skinny arms of yours?"

"Sure I can, if I lie down."

"Whoa! Whooooa!" "Hya-haah!"

The kids crowded around Sonia with excitement, but Cazze didn't even do that.

Did he think they were toys or something? Did he not know how dangerous guns were?

Pamela thought it might be one of those two, and yet staying silent didn't seem to be the best move, either. To begin with, she decided to figure out what was going through his mind.

"Um… Are you surprised?"

Cazze tilted his head, puzzled. He was still wearing that smile. "Hmm? About what?"

Something was off.

The boy's response planted a faint yet definite doubt in Pamela.

Something felt wrong. Just…overwhelmingly wrong.

A shiver ran down her spine.

Immediately understanding what that "something" was, she tried another question. "Cazze… What do you mean, 'with what'? You aren't frightened? There are so many guns here…"

"Huh?"

The boy's smile disappeared, as if he didn't understand what she was asking. He gave it a little thought, and then his eyes widened as if something had occurred to him. He nodded, smiling again. "Yes, I know they're dangerous."

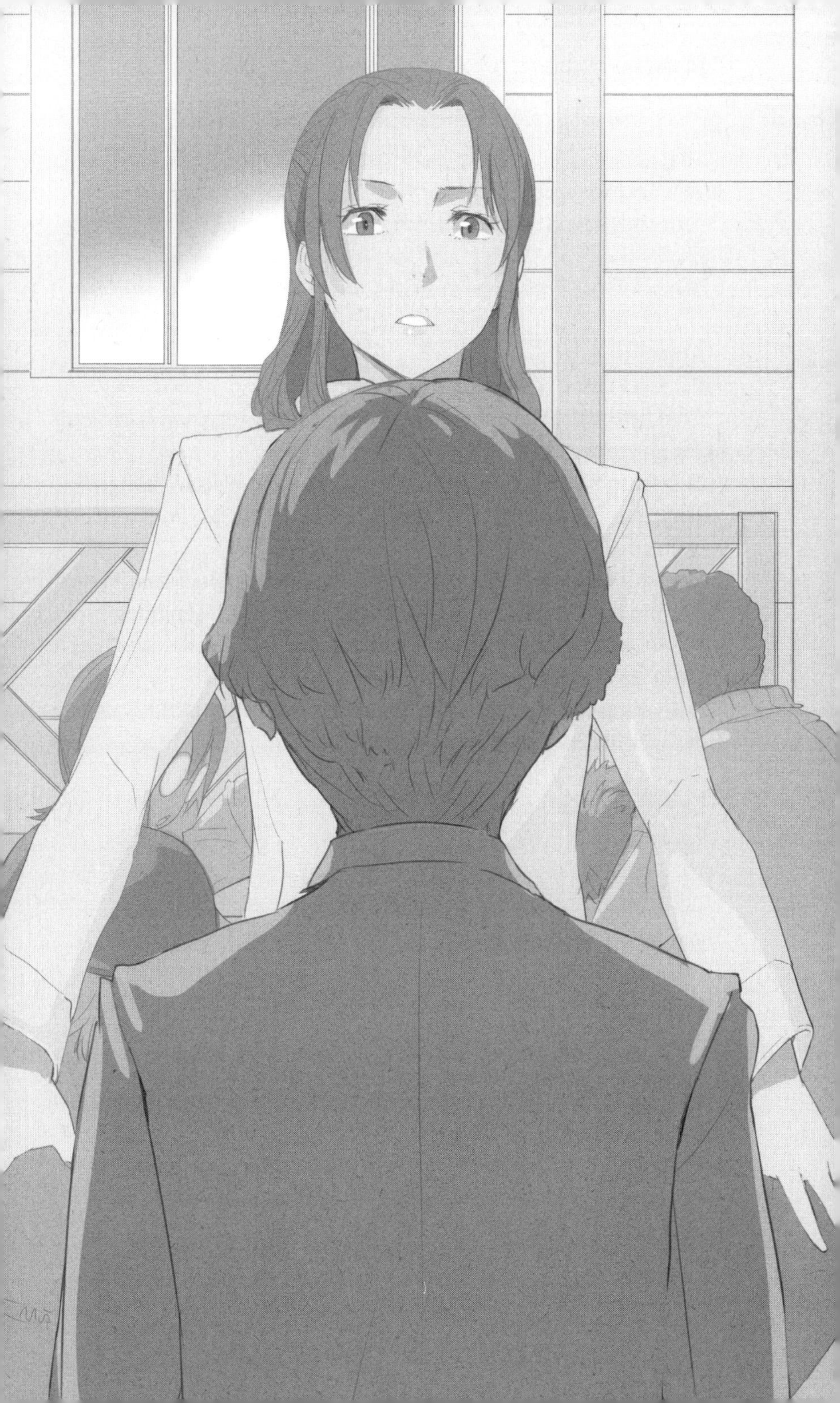

"…Huh? Oh, um…"

That answer seemed a little off base. For a moment, Pamela wasn't sure what to say, but then—

—the boy's next remark silenced her completely.

"They tell me I absolutely mustn't touch them until I'm *thirteen*!"

Krikk!

Pamela's spine creaked slightly.

Even before the words could strike her as odd, instincts born from her long years as a gambler spoke to her.

This wasn't a *Don't get in any deeper; it's dangerous* warning.

This time, her instincts were telling her, *It's too late, so brace yourself.*

Even so…

Even so, Pamela wanted to think that those instincts had been blunted by teaming up with Lana and distancing herself from gambling.

She hadn't realized that what had actually lost its edge was her, if she was trying to deny her instincts.

Delivering the coup de grâce, the boy spoke with a childlike smile and the brutality peculiar to children.

"All the people who work for us have *those*!"

⇔

The forest   Near the entrance

Pushing their motorcycles so that they could travel silently, the twin hunters were conversing calmly. They knew the "kidnappers" were armed now. If they rode their bikes, the noise of the engines would attract the enemy's attention, and there might also be a wire or some other trap on the road ahead.

They'd tried to torture their victim into revealing that information as well, but he'd blacked out, so they'd decided it was a waste of time and they should focus on securing Cazze.

"By the way, I, what weapons do I have ready?"

"Great question, Me. It's three handguns today, including backups."

"Two knives and wire. Just one gun."

"Packin' light, Me."

The two were talking as though this were an ordinary conversation, but the night was so late it was almost early again, and the forest was shrouded in eerie silence.

It wouldn't be too long before dawn broke.

They had to reach the bungalows before morning. On the other hand, that man had mentioned the kidnappers' main base. They could attack that first.

Still, that would be cutting it close.

After giving it a little thought, the politer of the twins spoke up. "Let's do this, I. You take all the money."

"Huh, so all the dough's coming over here, Me? Meaning…"

The polite twin got out his wallet and threw a leg over his bike. "Your brother will strike the headquarters by a different route. Take care of the transaction, I."

"On it, Me."

Taking the money, the coarse man spoke indifferently.

"If this ain't enough…we'll save the young master *by force*, then leave the rest of 'em six feet under."

⟺

Near the bungalows

Struck by self-loathing, Lana was immersed in solitary gloom.

"Aw, geez… Why am I like this?"

Thanks to her slip of the tongue, a group of passing train robbers had learned some information they absolutely didn't need to know. The fact that her group had also originally been planning to rob a train was giving her incredibly mixed feelings.

"That's right… We should have just stuck with the train robbery, like I planned. That way we wouldn't have had to mess with the kidnapping... Oh, it's not too late! We should hit that train!"

Switching moods in a heartbeat, Lana smartly straightened up and went around behind the bungalow.

Yes, all we have to do is use those young robbers! As a matter of fact, we can even piggyback on their heist, then flee in the confusion!

She obviously hadn't been listening to the part where the boys were going to steal the cargo without stopping the train. Lana clenched her fists and gave a quiet little shriek. "This will work!"

"Now that that's settled, the question is, What do we do with Cazze? Pamela isn't into the idea at this point, and neither am I. We can just leave him at the bungalow. That'll solve everything!"

Now that Pamela wasn't there to shoot down her ideas, the self-proclaimed criminal genius kept her brain running at full speed.

"Wait... The first and third bungalows have our footprints and fingerprints all over them. Oh, and are the other bungalows really empty? If somebody besides those kids has seen us, things could get ugly..."

Suddenly, both her mouth and her brain cells froze simultaneously.

There was only a little light from the moon and the lamp outside the bungalow, and Lana's surroundings were pretty gloomy.

Even so—she felt certain.

During her casual look around, she'd spotted two human figures between the bungalow and the woods, in a place that was usually out of sight.

They were about twenty yards away. If the bushes had been slightly thicker, she never would have noticed them.

After all, the pair were wearing what appeared to be military uniforms—and they were both lying flat on the ground.

"Huh... Who's that?"

She felt as if the core of her spine had turned to ice. Her legs started trembling, and she couldn't speak.

Bandits? Or are they the owners of the bungalows?

They can't be the police...right?

She hesitated, wondering whether she should call Pamela, but finally decided that they might be dummies or scarecrows. Trying to set her mind at ease, she took a step closer.

Then another.

And another.

With each step, she could see the figures more clearly. Their clothes didn't seem to be rumpled, and there were no obvious external wounds. Yet they lay perfectly still. She couldn't tell whether they were dead or just unconscious.

Focusing on the situation in front of her instantly sharpened her senses, and she began to pick up on something she hadn't noticed before.

What is that smell?

As she drew closer to the shapes on the ground, an odd odor began to steal into her nostrils.

It was a distinctive stench, like kitchen garbage. As if a whole lot of food had been left to rot.

Mingled with it was another, animal scent, like the fur of a wild dog.

What is this?

I feel a chill...

Her instincts must have noticed the abnormality nearby.

However, she'd missed one vital thing.

Beside the men's bodies, an enormous shadow was watching her from the darkness of the forest.

The shadow moved slowly, lumbering, but it was definitely getting closer to Lana.

Ten more feet to go. If the enormous shadow lunged, it would reach her in no time.

Lana still hadn't registered the oncoming shape.

Six feet.

The animal stink was getting stronger. Lana shivered. Slowly, she turned her head. She'd heard the sound of grass rustling.

Three feet.

She saw an enormous "shadow."

A gunshot rang out near the bungalows a moment later.

⟺

A few seconds earlier

"Okay, as a test, I'll shoot that broken branch!"

The moonlight illuminated a tree that was taller than the forest around it.

Sonia had spotted a branch that was broken in the middle, with one half dangling from the part that was attached to the trunk. It would do as a target.

It was quite a long way from where she stood, and she'd be aiming by moonlight. Even if she was wearing an army helmet, she was still a little girl. It was hard to see how she'd manage it, but Sonia took out a rifle, humming as she worked.

The guys started to place casual bets on whether she'd hit it or not, but—

—a gunshot rang out, and the broken half of the branch went spinning through the air.

Sonia staggered a little under the recoil, but she smiled when she saw that she'd hit her target. "Eh-heh-heeeh! I gooot it."

There was a moment of silence. Then the delinquents erupted into cheers.

"Hya-haah!"

"Hya-haw!"

"Whoa… Oh man… Wow! Just wooow!"

"She actually hit that thing!"

"Forget that—she actually fired that thing!"

"A skinny little kid like her! Unbelievable!"

"I haven't been that shocked since Jacuzzi was sobbing and blazing away with that machine gun!"

"That's incredible. The bullet went clean through that branch just 0.00023 seconds after she fired it."

"What the—?! Melody, you can tell?!"

"I said a random number, obviously."

"H-hey, you little—!"

"Encore! Encore!"

"Encore! Encore!"

"Encore! Encore!"

Rather nonsensical calls for an encore went up. A bit flattered, Sonia looked around for another target.

Just then, they all heard a scream.

From behind the bungalow, a short distance away, a woman's shriek pierced the quiet night.

Lana?! Pamela had been leaning against the truck's canvas back, but at the sound of that voice, she broke into a run before anyone else.

When she got there, panting for breath, she saw several things.

Lana had collapsed, foaming at the mouth. Two men in military uniforms were underneath her.

There was something else: odd, compressed patches in the grass, as though *something* had been standing there just a minute ago.

But that was all.

$$\Longleftrightarrow$$

In the forest

"…A gunshot?"

"It came from the direction of the bungalows, Comrade Sarges."

"I know that."

A gunshot had reverberated through the woods, taking them by surprise. The sound hadn't been that far away—most likely very close to the bungalows, Sarges determined. "Let's hurry," he said, keeping his cool. Something must have happened.

He walked faster, feeling a little irritated. *That sound… It wasn't the model my men use.*

I didn't hear anyone return fire, either.

Now entirely on his guard, the man *tsk*ed in frustration, thinking fast.

Dammit… Are you telling me someone got them?

*　　　*　　　*

We'll have to consider the possibility that the government's dogs are here.

⟺

In the forest

"……"

The twin who'd been put in charge of the handoff responded to the gunshot with silence, but his expression instantly hardened. Still pushing his motorcycle, he broke into a run.

If that had been the sound of someone shooting Cazze dead—

—he steeled himself to slaughter the enemy, then die himself.

⟺

Near the bungalows

He—Cookie—was startled.

The young people's cheers had drawn him out of the hut.

The air felt extremely cold, but the instincts from his circus days had won out. He'd been on his way toward the voices when he'd spotted two moving shadows.

His hunger hadn't driven him to make a meal of them.

Ever since he'd bitten that boy Claire's arm, he'd known that humans were poisonous.

Perhaps seeing some of them after all this time had made him feel nostalgic.

Maybe he'd remembered how he'd rushed at Claire and his trainers and knocked them over or rolled them around, and it made him want to experience that again.

There was no way to know for sure, but in any case, when Cookie sprang at the men, he had no intention of killing them.

That said, he'd made several miscalculations.

First, the people he'd jumped at in the past had been trained circus professionals.

Second, he was quite a bit larger than he had been when the circus broke up, and his weight had soared to match.

His torso squashed the Lemures flat—fortunately not lethally—and they blacked out instantly.

The sight startled Cookie. Memories of the past flashed through his mind.

Once, he'd lunged at a juvenile member of the troupe who was smaller than he was. The kid had been knocked out, and his trainer had given him a fearsome scolding.

It wasn't clear how much he understood of what he was seeing, but he did seem to remember that if the person he lunged at stopped moving, he got yelled at. Following his instincts, Cookie turned and went deeper into the woods.

Then, remembering that not one of the people who'd been there at the time—including Claire, the ringmaster, and his trainer—was here now, Cookie shuffled back.

Straight smack into a bespectacled human, just as he heard a gunshot.

What a nasty sound.

If Cookie had used language the way humans did, he probably would have thought those words.

He'd heard that noise in the woods many times before he was sold to the circus. He had clear memories of companions shaped like him and the "prey" who lived in the woods collapsing, one after another, when that sound rang out.

Then, when the circus fought with that group they'd called a gang, he'd heard the same noise—and one of the children who'd cheered for him had collapsed, blood streaming from his leg.

The people who were making those noises soon stopped moving, thanks to Claire and the ringmaster, but the cheers had died away, and an ugly silence had filled the tent.

Cookie loathed those sounds even more after that.

I hate that noise.

With a quiet, wary growl, he fled down the road behind the bungalows.

Cookie, an enormous monster, was running like a bunny.

Lana watched the enormous *thing* that had loomed up in front of her take off just as suddenly.

For a little while, she trembled, not understanding what had happened.

Once whatever it was was completely out of sight, she managed to scream.

⇔

Drawn by Lana's scream, everyone ran around the back of the bungalow. Meanwhile, Cookie ran around the front.

No one was there, though, and the cheers he'd heard a moment earlier had fallen silent.

Their scent was everywhere, and he couldn't even track them properly.

However, he spotted something familiar.

It was a big truck with a canvas back, the same sort the circus had used to travel.

There was another, smaller truck parked beside it, but Cookie ignored it and shambled over to the big one. Either because he was drawn to the familiarity or because he couldn't take the chill of the night wind anymore, he crawled into the back.

Inside the sheltered bed, he curled up quietly, and…

…wishing he could hear those cheers again, he slowly closed his eyes.

If grizzlies dreamed, he was definitely dreaming about the circus right then.

Of his days in the bed of a truck, traveling to all sorts of different places with Claire and his circus companions.

⇔

A few minutes later   Near the bungalows

"I-it's true! Believe me!"

"Well, um… It's less that I don't believe you than that I have no idea what I'm supposed to believe. What happened?"

"It was here! Something was here!"

"What do you mean, 'something'?"

"I mean *something*!"

Although Pamela had managed to wake Lana up from her faint, she wasn't making any sense.

She said she'd been attacked by something enormous, but she wasn't injured, and no one had seen anything suspicious when they checked around the bungalows.

Still, given the two unconscious mystery men, they decided it couldn't hurt to be careful.

"Who do you suppose these army types are anyway?"

"I don't know! Maybe they came to hunt deer? N-never mind them—is that…that…huge something really not around anymore?!"

"For now, yes. So calm down a little, all right?"

Unlike Lana, the men in military uniforms had actually been hurt, and it might be a while before they regained consciousness. Pamela and Lana couldn't just leave the people there, so they'd temporarily relocated them to the bed of their truck.

Meanwhile, the guys had already started preparing to leave the bungalow.

They were having to scramble after Melody said, "At the earliest, that train will be coming through in another thirty-three minutes and thirty-two seconds. We'll need to move soon!"

*   *   *

"So hey, couldn't we just go after the train's passed through? I'm still sleepy."

"Nah, Jacuzzi and the other guys said they were going to make sure our boats were there before they dropped the cargo. We need to be there."

"Jacuzzi's plan sure is a pain in the ass. If they'd grabbed the cargo before the train left, we wouldn't need to go to all this trouble."

"How would they steal it?"

"Couldn't they have Donny pick up the train and throw it?"

"You think Donny's strong enough for that?!"

"If he was, he wouldn't need us to make a living!"

The guys' conversation was as mindless as usual, and Melody rang her bells, warning them. "Listen up: We've got thirty-two minutes and fifty seconds left. It'll take us about five minutes to drive there, so we have to give ourselves some extra time."

"I guess so, huh…"

The eastern sky was starting to pale, but the stars still shone above their heads. In the midst of a beautiful forest scene, the delinquents bustled around, preparing to leave.

"Damn, it's cold."

"I bet it'll be even colder out on the river."

"Yeah, if it gets cloudy, we're definitely gonna see snow."

"Let's borrow a ton of blankets from the bungalows. We can fold 'em and return 'em on our way back," somebody suggested.

Everybody was in favor, and they began hauling all the blankets outside. This was a crime whether they returned them or not, but nobody present had enough of a moral compass to care in the first place. The one guy who probably would have been against it and managed to stop them was currently on the train, smack in the middle of a major incident. However, the delinquents didn't know that, and they began loading the blankets onto their truck without a care in the world.

"Whoa, what? I thought I was the first one, but there's already a good pile in here." The boy who'd carried the first blankets in gave a disappointed sigh.

There was a heap of brown in the back of the gloomy truck. That was what it looked like to the kid anyway, and he tossed the new blankets on top of the brown ones.

The other delinquents followed his lead, piling more and more blankets on top of the others.

"? It smells kinda like dog back here."

"I bet it's the blankets. People probably let their hunting dogs curl up in 'em, too."

"Huh. Well, it's not like we can be picky!"

In the end, nobody saw the pile of blankets shift a little—

—and the "heap of brown blankets" let the warmth of the fabric that had been piled on top of him nudge him toward sleep.

Drowsily, drowsily…

⇔

In front of Bungalow Number 3

The kid is by the bridge, with some boys who were passing by. Put the money in this crate and float it down the river.

"That should do it."

Writing the note on a piece of paper, Pamela took a crate from their truck, emptied it, put the note inside, and set it by the bunga-low's entrance. "Now let's hope this throws them off…"

"What are you talking about, Pamela? What about the huge something?"

Pamela sighed quietly, interrupting Lana's frightened questions. Her expression was serious. "The shape you saw concerns me…but something else is scaring me more, Lana."

"Wh-what?! There's nothing scarier than that huge thing! I guar-antee it!" Lana said emphatically.

Ignoring her, Pamela went on calmly. "Listen. I remembered something about Cazze's family. Or rather, I was reminded of it a minute ago."

"Wh-what?"

Cazze had already climbed into the bed of the truck with Sonia. Turning back to check one more time, Pamela went on in a whisper. "I remembered the name 'Runorata.'"

"? What's Runorata?"

"…It's Cazze's last name! At least remember that much!"

"Oh— Ohhhh! Yes, that's right! Of course I remember that! I was just testing you—ow-ow-yow-ow-ow-ow-ow!"

Pinching Lana's cheek, Pamela sighed and went on. "The Runorata Family."

"Huh?"

"They're one of the biggest mafia syndicates in the East. They never show up out West, but they're a pretty notorious gang on this coast. Not that I know any details."

"A—a gang?" Lana's eyes widened.

Pamela gave a wry smile that was pretty close to resignation. "Right. Which means, that big old mansion is built on a whole lot of crimes—and when we said not to call the cops, do you know what we basically told them? '…Don't hand us over to the police. Judge our crime by your own standards.'"

"……"

Pamela's sober words had made even Lana absorb the situation. She turned even paler than she had when she saw the "something," and her teeth chattered audibly. "In other words… Um, wait, what? If they catch us…"

"They'll cut off all our fingers, yank out all our teeth, bore out our eyes, then kill us."

Lana almost screamed, but Pamela covered her mouth. The look in her eyes said she was already bracing for certain death.

"…And if we're lucky, that's *all* they'll do."

⇔

Once she'd finished getting ready, Pamela pushed a pale, frightened Lana into the passenger seat, then climbed into the driver's seat.

Lana gazed up at the ceiling of the cab as if she felt sick. Finally, she spoke, sounding tired. "By the way...what are we going to do with those hunters? Their pulses and everything were normal, right?"

The soldier types showed no sign of waking. They were still in the bed of the truck.

There hadn't been space to lay both men down, so they'd propped one up against the canvas side in a sitting position. They'd opened the back to let fresh air in; if they'd driven through a town, they probably would have provoked a few questions. Out here in the woods, though, there wouldn't be anyone to see them.

"That doesn't mean we can just leave them. For now, we'll take them to the river. If they still don't wake up, we'll take them to a doctor later. Will that work?"

"...Yeah. Oh, you know, I don't have the spare brainpower to think about this stuff."

"What a coincidence. Me either."

Maybe because she was preoccupied with thoughts of the Runoratas, Pamela had treated the two men rather carelessly.

If they happened to be the bungalows' real owners, they could probably just say they'd gotten lost and had borrowed a hut for the night. The men seemed very odd for soldiers, and their guns weren't suitable for a hunting trip. She'd taken the bullets out, though, and Sonia was currently having fun keeping an eye on the weapons.

"Still, if they aren't hunters, I wonder if they're real soldiers. Maybe their training was too harsh and they deserted, then collapsed here... Or they could be mafiosi who came to pay the bounty—to kill us— so I've tied their arms and legs. Nothing too intense, though."

"You're surprisingly thorough about that sort of thing."

"I don't want to risk leaving them when we don't know what their deal is, that's all." Pamela slowly put their truck in gear, following the delinquents' two trucks. "Now, then... I hope we manage to convince them we got threatened into making a phone call by a mysterious kidnapper..."

*   *   *

They were going to the river with the delinquents because she'd decided that the bigger the group, the less likely it was that the mafia would just shoot them dead. It would mean dragging the delinquents into it, but those kids weren't ordinary citizens, either. They were train robbers. Just as traveling companions made the trip, the success of evil deeds depended on who you were with, and she planned to make the best possible use of the group.

Pamela wasn't a good person by any stretch of the imagination, and although it pricked her conscience a little, she made up her mind to use them.

She understood that both the delinquents and her own group were like rabbits wandering the desert.

They couldn't see what was around them. Their pasts were a desiccated wasteland, and they had nowhere to go.

That meant they had to keep searching for an oasis, at least.

A rabbit that lost its goal in life would soon disappear into the sand.

It was a lonely thought, but Pamela accepted its harsh truth with clear eyes. Quietly, she stepped on the gas.

The delinquents and the bandit gang left the bungalows behind them.

The rattletrap truck carried a bomb named Cazze.

One of the big trucks held another bomb named Cookie.

They simply drove on, bound for the foot of the bridge.

⟺

In the woods

On the way to the river, the three trucks passed a group of Lemures led by Sarges.

The occupants of the trucks didn't notice them; Sarges's group had heard their engines and promptly hidden in the forest.

As they watched the vehicles pass by, the men in military uniforms whispered to one another.

"Those trucks… Think they're those kids from yesterday?"

"Probably."

"What happened…? They don't look like government dogs, but…"

The mere fact that they had come this way meant that the pair who'd gone on ahead had failed in their mission.

They didn't seem to be armed. By all appearances, they were a group of common thugs. However, in the unlikely event that they actually had weapons, the Lemures' group might not be big enough to deal with them all.

There could be National Guard troops or Beriam's private soldiers in the backs of those trucks; the Lemures couldn't act carelessly.

"Well, unless that smoke signal goes up, Beriam's daughter will die either way… Hmm?"

The last truck was more run-down than the others. As it passed them, they noticed a certain anomaly.

One of their comrades who'd been sent ahead as a scout was sitting in the truck bed, propped up against the canvas cover. He didn't seem to be bleeding, but they couldn't tell whether he was alive or dead.

Sarges restrained his men until the truck was gone. Then he murmured without emotion, "No matter what else they may be…they're clearly our enemies.

"We're turning back. We'll find out what they are, then eliminate them."

⇔

Beside the bridge

The two Lemures who'd stayed behind were talking next to their tent.

"What sort of trouble is it anyway?"

"Search me. As long as we manage to convey our intentions to the other group, though, we shouldn't have any problems."

The pair were discussing the operation to retake Huey Laforet, which was currently underway.

"I feel bad for the kid, though. How old are we talking, ten or so?"

"Don't trouble yourself about it. Growing up under the protection of a rich, powerful parent has a price. We're about to deliver the bill—that's all."

"True. The kid's fated to die whether or not the negotiations succeed."

"Ha! Can you even call that a hostage?"

They were talking about a girl named Mary Beriam, who was tied up on the train. Unfortunately for them, though, a man was eavesdropping from the shadows under the trees, and their conversation ended up provoking him in a big way.

"Hey."

""Huh? Wha—?!""

At the sudden voice behind them, the two men turned around simultaneously, and—

—taking a thumb to the throat at the exact same time, they both blacked out.

Granted, when they woke up a few minutes later, they'd undergo torture so rapid and effective that they'd wish they were dead.

"You were planning to kill the young master either way...?

"You kidnappers are hilarious. We'll take a hundred days each to kill you."

Digression

Bartolo Runorata, the don of the Runorata Family, always had a security team of twelve guards.

The group was split into three units of four members each. The teams guarded Bartolo himself and his family by turns, with one team off duty at all times.

While the guards were off duty, absolutely no one could make them work.

Not even Bartolo Runorata.

Gabriel and Juliano, twin brothers affiliated with that security team, were off duty when Cazze was kidnapped. However...

"Mr. Bartolo. Would you let Me and I handle that mission?"

"Since this is young Master Carzelio, of course I and Me should be the ones who do it."

Gabriel spoke formally, while Juliano came off as rougher.

The pair called each other I and Me, a quirk that occasionally made conversations confusing; however, they always worked as a team, and most of the people around them saw them as "two in one."

They'd been assigned to the security team when Carzelio—Bartolo's first grandchild—was born, and they were often charged with guarding and taking care of him.

At first, Gabriel and Juliano had thought, *We should be risking our lives to protect Bartolo, not his family.* But the security team veterans had told them that they should consider Mr. Bartolo's family part of him, so they'd continued to carry out their guard duties mechanically.

They'd changed their minds when a dozen toughs had attacked Cazze just after he turned five.

⟺

Several years earlier

"…We were told to do our best not to let the young master witness any killing, I."

"Not even possible, Me. We did do our best, for five seconds or so."

Standing in front of the car that held Carzelio and his father, Gabriel and Juliano cracked their necks.

The ground around them was littered with dead thugs.

Spattered with their victims' blood, the twins looked like demons who'd crawled out of hell.

"……"

Carzelio's father had married into the family, and the sudden attack and subsequent carnage had left him speechless. He was still showing quite a bit of courage; any ordinary person would have been curled up in a ball, screaming.

However—when Carzelio abruptly opened the car's door and stepped out, he spoke to them with such an *innocent* smile. "Um… Ummm… Gabriel, Juliano, thank you very much!"

Carzelio's eyes were shining as if he were looking at heroes from the comic books.

It was just a brief expression of gratitude.

That remark from a guileless child seemed terribly out of place here, surrounded by the stench of iron and splashes of dark red.

Nevertheless, the words definitely touched their hearts.

The pair had been called mad dogs, and everyone except for Bartolo had eyed them with fear and hatred.

This boy had seen their brutality. The smells of blood and gunsmoke

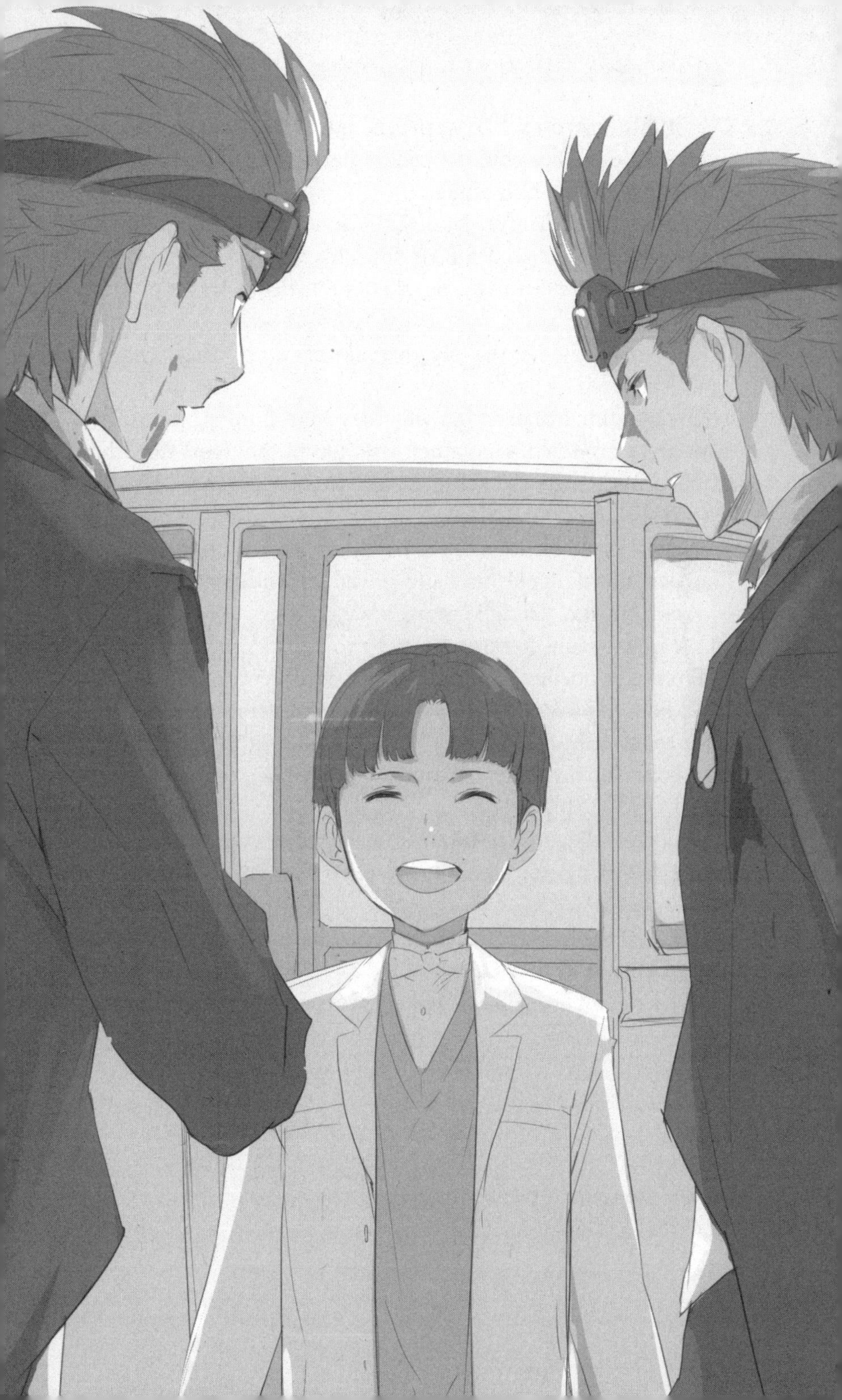

were in his nostrils, yet he wasn't the least bit scared. He genuinely thanked them. They couldn't believe he was real. They both stood there stunned for a little while.

"Young master. You're not afraid?" Juliano was still holding his gun, his victims' blood dripping down his face.

Carzelio cocked his head, puzzled as to what he was supposed to be frightened of.

The twins looked at the boy, then at each other. They broke into blood-spattered smiles.

Carzelio didn't understand why they were smiling, and he grew even more mystified. His father, who found the twins disturbing, grabbed his son by the scruff of the neck and dragged him back toward the car.

The twins paid no attention to the man's reaction. In perfect sync, they went down on one knee and bowed their heads to Cazze.

"We thank you, young Master Carzelio."

"We were simply doing our duty by you. Just doing our job."

"From now on, our loyalty is not only for Mr. Bartolo."

"To both I and Me, you are our rightful master as well."

The twins delivered this speech by turns, alternating lines. Carzelio's eyes shone, and his father's eyebrows drew together, but that was all.

From that day on, a certain rumor began to circulate within the Runorata Family: An innocent sovereign had tamed two mad dogs in an instant.

It seemed the battle to decide the great Bartolo Runorata's successor had already been decided.

…That rumor brought a complicated grimace to Carzelio's father's face.

$$\Longleftrightarrow$$

And now—

Even though the two were off duty, they'd asked Bartolo to give them the mission of rescuing Carzelio.

"...You're not working today. I don't have the authority to give you an order," Bartolo told them.

"Quite so," Gabriel said. "That said...while we are off duty, provided we don't oppose the Runorata Family, we may do whatever we like. I believe that was the rule."

"You're correct." Bartolo nodded easily, and Juliano picked up the conversation.

"In other words, I and Me aren't guards right now. We're hunters, using our day off on a side gig."

"Are you now?"

"If we've earned your confidence, Master Bartolo Runorata, would you please hire us?"

Bartolo gave the somewhat melodramatic pair an intimidating look. Then, noting that their gazes hadn't wavered in the slightest, he sighed.

"No need for any more theatrics.

"Plus, you know security is the side gig. Hunting is your main occupation."

⇔

The two hunters were unleashed a few minutes later.

They were hounds—or maybe mad dogs.

They were also first-class hunters.

Each hunter would scare his prey, then sink his fangs into its throat.

They sang their hunting song—proud to be able to protect their other master, and enjoying their work.

They sang against the music of motorcycle engines and sharpened their fangs to fine points.

They had no idea what sort of chaos waited for their song, their bikes, and their malice.

Final Chapter   **Neither Hare nor There**

Beside the river

"Okaaaay, we're here!"

"Awright! Unload the boats!"

"Twenty-one minutes and thirteen seconds left."

The boys were acting like kids on a camping trip, and reaching the river had given them an extra shot of energy. Even the sleepier ones all jumped up, stuck their feet in the cold December river, and ended up yelling "Hya-haah, hya-haah," in an imitation of Chaini. Melody and the few other members who'd kept their cool watched them with chagrined smiles.

Meanwhile, Pamela and Lana had stopped their truck a short distance away, but they didn't get out.

Sonia and Cazze had already clambered out of the bed and were goofing around with the delinquents. It had only been half a day, but the pair really seemed to have hit it off. Although she was five-plus years older than he was, Sonia looked more like Cazze's friend than his big sister.

"So wh-what do we do? Take Sonia and run?"

"If we do that, they'll definitely treat the delinquent robbers as the kidnappers."

"…Wasn't that what you were planning on?"

"I'm on the fence about it. If they were regular joes who had nothing to do with this, it wouldn't even be an option. They're train robbers, though, which means they're like us. But then again, they didn't get in our way... I just don't know what to— Wait a second." Suddenly, Pamela fell silent. She opened the window, straining her ears.

"Wh-what's the matter, Pamela?"

"Just now...I thought I heard somebody scream."

⟺

"Hmm... Someone's here. Did they hear you scream?"

The twin struck sharply at the stomachs of the men he'd been torturing, summarily knocking them out and ending their pain prematurely.

He hid the pair behind a car parked some distance away. Then, slipping into the shadows under the trees, he watched for approaching figures.

Sure enough, two appeared.

A pair of young women who seemed to have no connection to the military men.

⟺

As the two of them got out of the truck and took a good look at the woods, they saw something that appeared to be sooty fabric up ahead, partway up the slope that led to the bridge. Realizing it was part of a tent, they slowly started climbing the hill, through the trees—and discovered several cars, parked where they couldn't be seen from below.

"What...is this?" Pamela looked around, but she didn't hear any more screaming.

The tent wasn't the sort used for camping. It was a large military tent, with a metal frame and a low roof. Inside, there was a folding table and several chairs, with what appeared to be a detailed code chart open on the table. A wireless set was sitting on top of a car. This obviously wasn't a group of ordinary campers or birdwatchers.

"Blood...?"

The stain was on a corner of the tent. Chills raced down the women's spines. Lana's glasses rattled on her nose, and Pamela squeezed her hands into fists.

"I-it's that thing...! That—that huge black shadow did this!"

She wanted to tell Lana that was ridiculous, but even with all this equipment here, there wasn't a soul to be seen. Only that bloodstain remained.

Under the circumstances, it would have been understandable even for people who weren't Lana to suspect the supernatural.

"...Let's go back, Lana. I'm worried about the others."

"Y-yes, you're right... But that huge shadow... There's no telling whether Sonia's guns will even work on— Hmm?" When she averted her eyes from the bloodstain, Lana had noticed something odd on the opposite side of the tent, in a corner.

It was a white tube, with a pin attached to one bulging end.

"A hand grenade!" Lana snatched it up and turned back to Pamela, her eyes shining. "If we have this, we might be able to kill that huge thing if it shows up! Luck is on our side!" She gave a firm thumbs-up.

Pamela met it with an endlessly weary look.

She didn't go along with her, but she also didn't reproach her for stealing the grenade. Keeping a wary eye on their surroundings, she turned back and began to retrace their steps.

"Let's go. I'm worried about Cazze and Sonia."

Waiting until the pair had started down the hill, a man poked his head out from behind a tree. "Those women... One of them just used young Master Carzelio's nickname..."

After a little hesitation, the man decided to silently follow the women.

⇔

The riverbank

The delinquents had finished lining the boats up on the shore, and now they were horsing around, soaking their feet in the midwinter river as if they didn't know the meaning of the word *cold*.

Cazze didn't want to get his trousers wet just so he could feel chilled, and he was having fun watching the other kids from the bank.

Then one of the boys got careless, slipped, and fell right into the water. "Gwuff?! ...C-cooOOOoold!"

"Hya-haah!" "Hya-haw!"

"What's that hya-haw-ing about?! Huh?! What about me freezing my butt off is worth a hya-haw?! Dammit! W-wait, my shoes, where'd my shoes go?!"

The guy started yelling at Chaini and company, but the chill cooled his head down fast, and he realized he had bigger things to worry about.

He'd shucked his shoes off on the shore, but they had since been washed away. Then he spotted them snagged on the bank quite a ways downstream. Clambering into a nearby boat, he shouted at several people on the shore who still had their shoes on. "Hey! I'm just gonna go grab my shoes! Somebody go get a blanket from that pile in the truck! I c-can't take this cold!"

The boy sneezed, but almost nobody was listening to him. Even the ones who only laughed heartlessly and said, "Go get it yourself."

But Cazze heard the kid's shouts and spoke up happily. "I'll get you one!"

"Hey, thanks! I'm counting on ya!"

The delinquents had only just met this boy, who also happened to be an oblivious kidnapping victim, and yet they were casually using him as a gofer. They didn't mean any harm, though. They'd genuinely accepted Cazze into their circle.

Their relaxed attitude was totally new to Cazze. He'd never been treated like this before, but it didn't bother him.

In fact, it was what he'd longed for from the bottom of his heart.

He didn't understand why he felt exhilarated. He was simply happy that these older boys, whom he'd just met, were treating him like one of their own. Smiling, he climbed into the bed of the truck.

And with that smile still on Cazze's face...

...in that supposedly deserted truck, he came face-to-face with *him*.

⇔

Once again, Cookie had been drawn up from a deep sleep into a shallow one.

As the truck bounced and rattled along, he'd heard the boys and girls being noisy. It had reminded him of the excitement from his circus days and started to bring his temperature back up.

That had ended, and he'd nearly fallen asleep again, but someone began to shake his back. Still half asleep, Cookie raised his head and poked it out of the mound of blankets. He turned to look around.

And faced a boy.

⇔

A bear.

Cazze might have been raised as a bird in a cage, but even he knew what this was.

It was a unique individual, quite a bit larger than an ordinary grizzly, but he probably didn't know that.

Still, a bear. A bear through and through. Overwhelmingly grizzly. Heartbreakingly grizzly.

This situation was tailor-made for such dramatic expressions.

The small face of a boy who wasn't yet ten years old stared right at the hairy face of a bear three times his width—and that was ignoring any other measurements. Someone with a weak heart could easily have died of shock on the spot. Even if they didn't, they would have had to prepare to die for a different reason.

The boy was lucky on two fronts, though.

First: The bear was very *used* to humans and didn't see them as food.

Second: When it came down to it, the boy was a *Runorata*.

"Wow! I've never seen one of these before!"

As he spoke, Cazze began *petting* the bear's cheeks.

Anyone with common sense would have considered this completely abnormal.

Who could say for sure that it was due to his innocence and ignorance? A creature with sharp fangs and claws, something more than twice the size of a human, was right there in front of the boy. Even so, that overwhelming "beastly presence" didn't faze the kid at all. He just ran his fingers through its fur gently, as if it were a pet dog or cat he'd had for years.

"Incredible! This... This is what it's like being outside...!"

Young as he was, Cazze felt an odd surge of deep emotion, and he put it into simple words.

"Outside" was a vague concept, but the young boy was outside and free for the first time in his life, and it was probably the best he could do.

Meanwhile, the boy's delighted voice seemed to have reassured Cookie, who pushed his snout into the boy's own cheek.

"Ah-ha-ha! That tickles!"

The child didn't seem to feel any wariness toward him at all. He reminded Cookie of the redheaded kid. The grizzly kept his eyes on the boy's face, and in it, he caught glimpses of the good old days.

For a little while, Cazze was all excited about the creature he'd stumbled onto. Then he remembered why he was here and hastily grabbed a blanket. "I forgot," he told the bear. "I'm sorry—I have to take this to him! See you later, Mr. Bear!"

The bear tilted his head, looking rather lonely, but he didn't try to keep the boy there.

That's amazing! I made lots of friends...and I met a real live bear! Cazze thought as he headed out of the truck.

Was it because he'd grown up with the intimidating Bartolo? When it came to feeling fear, the boy's skin was extremely thick. Awed by his miraculous communion with the bear, he climbed down from the truck and broke into a run.

Yet another unexpected thing happened to the guileless boy.

*   *   *

The truck wasn't far from the riverbank.

Clutching the blanket, the boy started to call to the delinquents—

—but an arm suddenly snaked around his neck and cut him off.

A gunshot echoed through the woods by the river, terribly out of place in the peaceful environment.

⇔

"What's up?" "Hya-haah?" "Hya-haw."

When the gunshot rang out, everyone who was down by the river turned around.

"...Hey, who're they?"

"Friends of the fellas that we found up by the bungalows, maybe?"

"Uh, guys? This is completely not the time!"

Five or six men in military uniforms were standing there. They were all holding guns. One of them had just fired his at the ground; fresh smoke drifted from its muzzle.

However, what had startled the boys wasn't the guns or the group in army uniforms.

It was the fact that their leader had grabbed Cazze.

"All right. First things first: There's something I need to tell you."

The man spoke impassively, but his left hand held Cazze firmly by the throat. His right hand held a knife, and he set its sharp, gleaming edge against the boy's neck.

"Playtime is over, kids."

Sarges wasn't yelling, but his voice carried well.

The Lemures had opted to watch from beside the river for a while, and when a boy they assumed was the group's youngest member went off on his own, they'd grabbed the opportunity to take him hostage.

Now they began to interrogate the delinquents.

"Who exactly are you?"

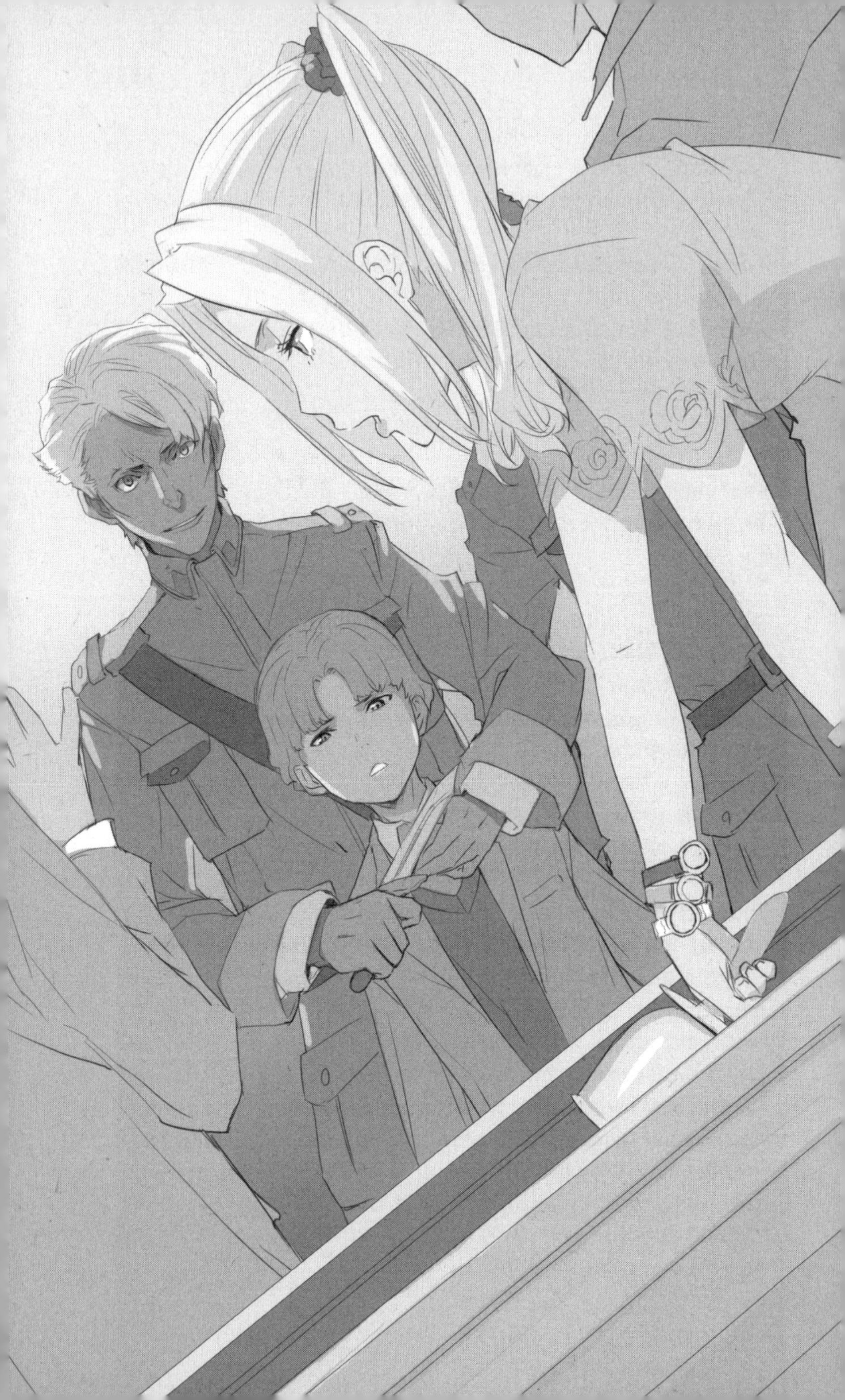

* * *

Sarges's dispassionate question clearly flustered the kids.

"Wha—?! Wait just a minute! 'Who are you?' That's what we wanna know!"

"Hey... They look like soldiers... Did they maybe find out about the freight robbery?"

"Wh-what do we do?!"

The boys whispered among themselves, but Melody ignored them and called to the man from the boat. Although her expression was still sleepy, her voice was dignified, if frightened.

"M-mister... We just came to check out the area downstream! We haven't done anything wrong, and we aren't planning to interfere with your soldiers' drill, so, um... Would you please let that boy go?!"

"Oh... You haven't done anything wrong, hmm?" With a flat chuckle, the group's uniformed leader shook his head. "Then how do you explain our unconscious comrades in the bed of that poor excuse for a truck?"

"That truck isn't ours, but...its owners found those men laid out by some bungalows, back in these woods! They said they were going to bring them to the river for some fresh air, and if that didn't wake them up, they'd take them to a hospital!"

Melody seemed completely different—far more deferential—and the boys exchanged looks.

"How is Melody managing to speak up like that?"

"She's good at this stuff; she kept herself fed by borrowing money, skipping out on the loans, and pickpocketing..."

"Forget that—seriously, what are those fellas? Nobody mentioned that the National Guard trained around here."

"Yeah, but they've got guns. Let's not tick them off."

The delinquents had mistaken the group for real soldiers. They held still as they watched the conversation unfold, careful not to do anything stupid, but then—

"Good grief. Do you really think we'll fall for that? Did you want me to shave this boy's nose off?"

"Nn—! Nnn——"

When they heard the military man's callous remark and saw that his grip on Cazze's throat was so tight that the boy could barely make a sound, the delinquents all spoke up in protest.

"Hold on! You fellas are soldiers, right?! Isn't protecting civilians your job?!"

"And even if you're mad at us, what did a little kid like him do?!"

The delinquents complained at him, but…

"You're still playing innocent? What fool would release a hostage because someone told him to? Although, as the situation stands, it doesn't look as if there's any real need for a hostage. We could just shoot all of you dead."

…when they saw Sarges's brutal smile, even the densest of the boys finally figured it out.

These men weren't soldiers. They were something much uglier and far more dangerous.

⇔

"Wh-what do we do, Pamela?! I knew those military types were bad news!"

"Quiet, Lana. They'll see us."

Pamela and Lana had been watching the scene on the riverbank from partway down the slope. Their timing had been good, and the men in uniform hadn't noticed them. As things stood, they could technically make their escape without getting dragged into the mess, but…

"What should we do? At this rate, they'll hurt Cazze!"

"If it comes down to it, I'll be a decoy. If we can at least save Cazze…"

From the sound of it, neither of them saw abandoning him to his fate as an option.

"…we'll risk it. If I can get to the truck, I'll be able to get the guns out of the bed. Then we can use those to—"

"I wouldn't be too hasty if I were you."

When the voice suddenly spoke behind them, Pamela and Lana tensed, all their hair standing on end. They steeled themselves, thinking a member of the military group must have snuck up on them from behind.

The figure who stood there was a young man whose clothes couldn't have been less appropriate for a forest by a riverbank. "Those men seem to have a decent amount of experience with guns. Amateurs who challenged them to a firefight would be unlikely to win it," he said. He was dressed entirely in black.

Pamela and Lana hadn't noticed him approaching. Not only that, but beneath his courteous words, they sensed an intimidating aura even greater than the group in military uniforms had.

And—his next words showed them that he most certainly wasn't their ally.

"Rescuing the young master unharmed isn't your job, in any case. That duty was assigned to Me and I."

The way he referred to himself was odd, but the man clearly had connections to the Runorata Family.

"Eep..."

"Don't."

Lana shuddered, reaching for the hand grenade she'd picked up a minute ago, but Pamela immediately held her back.

The man in black didn't even seem to see them anymore. He was watching the situation down by the river. "If only I had an opportunity of some sort, I could rush them... Hmm?"

The man seemed to have spotted something. He looked mystified.

"What...might that be?"

⇔

"Answer me! How did you incapacitate our comrades?" Sarge bellowed, convinced that he had an unshakable advantage. He was wearing a rather sadistic smile. *Huh. Apparently, they really are just a band of thugs. How did this scum manage to take out our scouts...?*

I am concerned that the first negotiator hasn't returned, but... In any case, we should dispose of about half of them. Dealing with a large group is too hard on the nerves.

He began to order his subordinates to cull half the brats, but then he froze, his smile fading. Something wasn't right.

......? ...What is this?

Their faces gave him a bad feeling.

The boys' expressions were as pale as they had been a moment ago, but their eyes weren't focused on his group.

What...are they looking at...?!

As he began to glance around, searching for the cause of their unease, several of the boys whispered among themselves.

"Uh, if you wanna know what happened to your guys... Um..."

Just as Sarges's gaze turned in the direction of the truck—

"I think...it was probably *that*."

And whether they wanted to or not, Sarges's group saw something surreal.

He stood on his hind legs, stretching as far as *he* could. At that point, *he* was taller than the truck.

What...is...this?

What am I looking at right now?

It was so huge it had to be some kind of joke. The timing with which it had arrived was nothing short of comical.

⇔

"Ah— Aaaaaaaaaaaaaaah! That—! That's it! That's what I saw earlier!" Lana screamed, shaking Pamela's shoulders violently.

A being that was nearly beyond comprehension had entered the fray, and Pamela forgot herself for a few seconds.

The shaking jump-started her mind again, and she grabbed Lana's head with both hands and held it tight. Pressing her forehead against the other woman's, she snapped, "What 'huge something'? That is a goddamn grizzly bear!"

"It was a 'huge something' in the dark!"

With that inane retort in her ears, Pamela turned to the man who'd stopped them a moment ago. "What are you going to... Huh?"

But the man in black was gone.

⇔

Is this some kind of joke?

For both Sarges and the other Lemures, the development had come completely out of left field.

When they encounter a truly unexpected situation, most people go blank for a moment. They need time to get their confusion under control, compare what they were seeing with reality, and figure out their next moves.

Had they originally come to vanquish a monster, no doubt that blank moment wouldn't have happened. They were already holding rifles and tommy guns, and they would promptly have fired them.

The same thing would have been true if the grizzly had been smaller, a size more in line with common sense.

However, when confronted with that ludicrous creature, even the well-trained Lemures went blank for a moment.

In the first place, their group hadn't been assembled for combat. They'd only been selected to negotiate with the government.

That said, when faced with the "red monster," most of their comrades on the train had also gone blank.

The blank lasted only a few seconds.

Even a bare handful of seconds could be fatal, though.

At least that was true for these men, in this case.

After all, they ended up caught between a bear that was still upset about that earlier gunshot, and a third party who'd recovered from his own blank faster than anyone present.

Cookie hadn't come outside intending to kill.

Just as the boy had left the truck, he'd heard that "nasty sound," the gunshot, and so he'd poked his head out to see where it was coming from.

There were several men out there, and they were holding the tools that made that unpleasant noise. Apparently, they'd made the boys stop cheering.

Convinced that those tools were the cause of all the trouble, Cookie may simply have been trying to knock them out of the men's hands.

At the very least, he seemed to be acting more out of fear of the terrible sound than hatred.

However, when an enormous grizzly tries to slap something out of a person's hand—for a mere human, it's the same as getting dragged into a tornado.

The gun was knocked high into the air, and its owner went flying as well, in a slightly different direction. He might have blacked out before he had time to scream; he flew several yards in silence before his back slammed into the riverbank.

He didn't seem to be dead, but he was clearly unconscious.

A single attack had rendered an armed man unable to fight.

The terror of that fact swept over the Lemures, yanking them back to reality.

But it was too late.

Far sooner than that, the man who'd barely flinched at the sight of the oversize grizzly had come up behind them.

"Wha… What are you do…ing…? Fi—"

With his hand still around Cazze's neck, Sarges started to scream for his men to fire. Before he could get the words out, though, he heard a groan behind him—*and the sound of an approaching engine in the woods* made his heart freeze again.

While everyone was focused on the enormous bear, the young man had knocked out two of the Lemures.

Just then, with excellent timing, his twin emerged from the woods on his motorbike.

A second man in black burst onto the riverbank, riding a motorcycle that had the wooden crate with Pamela's note on its cargo rack.

"Wha... Wha—?!"

Sarges's brain was refusing to process the situation. In the next
moment, intense pressure came to bear on the wrist of his knife
hand.

"Gah— Wha... Aaaaaouwaaaagh?!"

He understood instantly that someone had grabbed him there,
but as he tried to twist around to see who it was, he lost track of the
positions of the ground, the sky, his own right arm, and the rest of
him. His feet rose into the air, and he rotated, then slammed into the
ground. A jolt of pain ran all through him.

"Gahk...!"

As his vision warped and turned all the colors of the rainbow,
Sarges managed to make out a man in black who was toying with
the knife he'd just been holding. Behind the man, he spotted the boy
he'd been restraining three seconds earlier. The man in black was
standing between them, as if to protect the kid.

The man spoke in a voice that held the utmost respect. "Young
master, it isn't safe here. Please go down to the river, if you would."

"Gabriel!"

Gabriel smiled reassuringly at the boy.

Meanwhile, the man who'd ridden up on the motorcycle took a
look around. "What the hell is all this, Me?"

"Juliano!"

When the boy called his name, Juliano got off his bike, held his left
hand out to the side, and bowed as respectfully as a butler. "I'm glad
you're safe, young Master Carzelio."

When he saw that laid-back exchange, Sarges realized something.

None of the Lemures had a gun anymore.

He hadn't seen it happen, but around the time he was taken out,
the others seemed to have dropped their weapons as well. One of
his comrades was groaning with a knife stuck in his arm, while the
grizzly had immediately sent someone else flying: Another man had

been knocked in the opposite direction from the first one and was still lying where he'd fallen.

On top of that, the boy Carzelio had done as he was told and gone to join the other kids by the river, avoiding the possibility of being taken hostage again.

Ridiculous... Ludicrous, inconceivable!

The grizzly seemed to be satisfied with the situation, dropping back to all fours to comfortably watch the boys by the river.

What...the hell...is going on...? Sarges stared at the scene in complete shock.

Juliano spoke impassively. "With that taken care of, I don't know who you are or where you're from, but...you didn't think you could make an enemy of the Runorata Family and actually get anything out of it, did you? Huh?"

"Wh...what?"

The Runorata Family...?

The name had come up very abruptly, and Sarges almost relapsed into confusion. However, mobilizing all the knowledge left in his brain, he managed to come up with an answer of sorts. "I...I see...! So Bartolo Runorata *is Senator Beriam's loyal hound...* Did he tell you to come here and dispose of...us...?"

He started with conviction but trailed off partway through.

He'd picked up on intense murderous hostility from the twins.

"...This guy says some pretty funny stuff, Me."

"He does indeed, I."

"What did he just call Mr. Bartolo? The head of our beloved family?"

"Don't say it, I. Even hearing it would be disrespectful."

Their tones grew colder and colder, and Sarges felt the blood retreating into his core.

"Then what do we do, Me?"

"To avoid any further disrespect, I, it would be best to ensure he can never speak again."

The conversation could have been a joke, but they certainly didn't sound as if they were fooling around.

As the men approached, step by step, Sarges felt despair settle over him.

But then the tables turned again.

"Freeze!"

A yell split the air, along with the clicking of guns being cocked. When he looked in that direction, two more men in military uniforms had appeared and were leveling guns at the black-clad twins.

Both men were holding old-model submachine guns. They stepped closer, little by little, keeping a wary eye on the grizzly in the background.

"Comrade Sarges, are you all right?!"

"Who are these people?!"

Pamela, Lana, Sonia, and the delinquents all recognized the newcomers' faces.

They were the pair who'd been passed out behind the bungalow.

"Aaaah! Those are my guns!"

Sonia protested, but the uniformed men didn't hear her.

They'd come to in the bed of the truck, freed their hands and feet, then grabbed the nearest weapons and gone outside. Then they'd seen their comrades on the ground and that enormous grizzly. This was obviously no time to nurse their lingering aches and pains, and they'd promptly joined the fray.

Meanwhile, although the twins didn't feel as if their lives were in danger, a different worry occurred to them, and they began to converse in whispers.

"The situation may compel us to draw as well, I."

"They've told us to do our best not to let the young master see any killing until he turns thirteen…"

"We have shown him once before, though. Besides, if we hesitate, a stray bullet could fly his way."

"…Man, oh man, what a pickle."

⇔

"Oh, right! Now's our chance!"

As the situation around Pamela and Lana devolved, Lana's eyes suddenly sparkled. She took something out of her jacket.

"Wh-what's the matter?!"

"Cazze is out of harm's way! We can take out this bunch, the Runorata men, and that big bear all at once!"

No sooner had she spoken than Lana yanked the pin from the white grenade.

"Huh?! W-wait a second, Lana!!"

If we do that, we'll make enemies of the Runoratas for sure—

Pamela reached out to stop Lana, but she was too late.

Lana had already flung the grenade.

⇔

A few of the uniformed men who could still move had gotten to their feet and were beginning to retrieve their guns.

"Heh...heh-heh. Pet dogs to a loyal hound, hmm? What a sloppy endgame," Sarges said, shooting them a leer. He was ready to demonstrate how thoroughly the tables had turned.

Despite his words, the situation flipped for a third time.

Clang, clang! Rattle, rattle, rattle...

A white cylinder came flying in out of nowhere and landed in the center of the commotion with a dry clatter.

Sarges recognized the object.

It was, in a way, the most important article in this operation.

Inconceivable.

What's the smoke flare *doing—?*

Before he could even think the rest of his question, a vast cloud of smoke billowed up.

⇔

"Whoa, whoa, whoa, whoa, hold up—what's going on here?"

"Bears, guns… Hey, is this part of the country supposed to have bears?!"

"L-look, what're we supposed to do with all this?!"

"Well, only two hundred and eighty-three seconds have passed since that gunshot."

"N-nah, that's got nothing to do with…"

"Hya-haah…" "Hya-haw…"

All Melody and the rest of the delinquents could do was watch the rapidly shifting situation from the sidelines.

"Still… That's a heckuva lot of smoke…"

"Might even be smokier than Miz Nice's smoke bombs, don'tcha think?"

The "grenade" Lana had thrown was a smoke flare the Lemures had planned to use to communicate the results of their negotiations to the train. It was something Huey Laforet had made for fun, and it really packed a punch; white smoke blanketed the area with the force of a minor explosion.

Sarges stood at the center of a pale wall stretching up and up, high into the air.

W-wait! Beriam hasn't accepted our demands…! he screamed internally, but it was too late.

As if celebrating its own birth, the smoke rose rapidly into the lightening predawn sky.

Regardless, the way things were going on the Flying Pussyfoot just then, smoke signals meant absolutely nothing.

⇔

Chaos took over.

Cookie didn't understand the situation at all, and it hadn't interested him in the first place. Not until the smoke shot into the air, and he sprang to his feet.

He was remembering his grand entrances at the beginning of the circus.

He'd run through dense billows of smoke: an enormous grizzly bursting out of the clouds, carrying a redheaded boy on his back.

Remembering that trick he used to always do, Cookie bounded happily to his feet and leaped into the expanding cloud of smoke.

⟺

"H-hey, we can't shoot like this! We'll hit each other!"

"Calm down! For now, circle around to the other side and get that grizzly first..."

The speakers were the pair who'd helped themselves to Sonia's guns, but they didn't get to finish their conversation. Before they had time to aim, a huge mass of fur burst through the smoke and charged gleefully toward the men, who were frozen with terror.

"AAAAAaaaaaaah!"

It squashed their screams right along with them, and they ended up reliving the tragedy that had occurred behind the bungalow.

However, they took 30 percent more physical damage this time.

⟺

By the time Pamela and Lana timidly made their way down the hill, everything was over.

The twins in black had taken advantage of the smoke to completely steamroll the Lemures and were piling the unconscious men into a heap.

As the two crept closer, they began to hear the twins' conversation.

"Still, what was that all about, Me? 'Put the money in the crate'? It makes no sense," Juliano said.

Gabriel gave a wry smile. "We'll go over the details later, I. Your brother tortured some of them earlier and got them to spill their objective."

"Hmm? Their objective? Wasn't it kidnapping the young master, Me?"

"No, apparently they were after the train that's about to pass through here."

"Huh?" Juliano seemed lost. Roughly tossing an unconscious military man onto the pile, he glanced at Gabriel again. "So they weren't the kidnappers, Me?"

"Mm... That's an excellent question, I. They did say the caller was a woman," Gabriel murmured. Smiling, he turned to look back at Pamela and Lana.

"Eep!"

This is bad.

Are they onto us?

Although Pamela had braced for death earlier, the man's smile made her knees go watery with terror. Even so, she didn't let it show on her face.

Before she could say a word, though, Juliano cracked his neck. "Nice work, dollface. That smoke screen back there really helped us out. Didn't it, Me?"

"Yes, it truly was helpful. Oh, that's right, I: Go and retrieve the young master, please. There are no more enemies."

"Whoops, good catch."

The man ran over to the group of boys by the river, who were watching them with worry. After his twin had gone, Gabriel quietly turned to face Pamela and Lana. "Now, then... I suppose I should ask, who are you? You really can't have been 'just passing through' way out here."

Well, now. Will we be able to fool him? That really is the gamble of a lifetime, isn't it? Summoning her courage, Pamela drew in a deep breath. If it came down to it, she was prepared to take all the blame.

Before she could say anything, Lana started apologizing with tears in her eyes. "I'm sorry... I'm so sorry! It was me! Cazze got into the back of our truck, and I came up with the idea of kidnapping him!"

"Wha...?! L-Lana?!"

Lana had caved to their intimidating opponent and spilled the whole truth immediately. Pamela's eyes went round, and all the excuses she'd come up with evaporated.

Even as Lana spilled all the details of what had happened, she didn't mention Pamela or Sonia once. "B-but none of the other

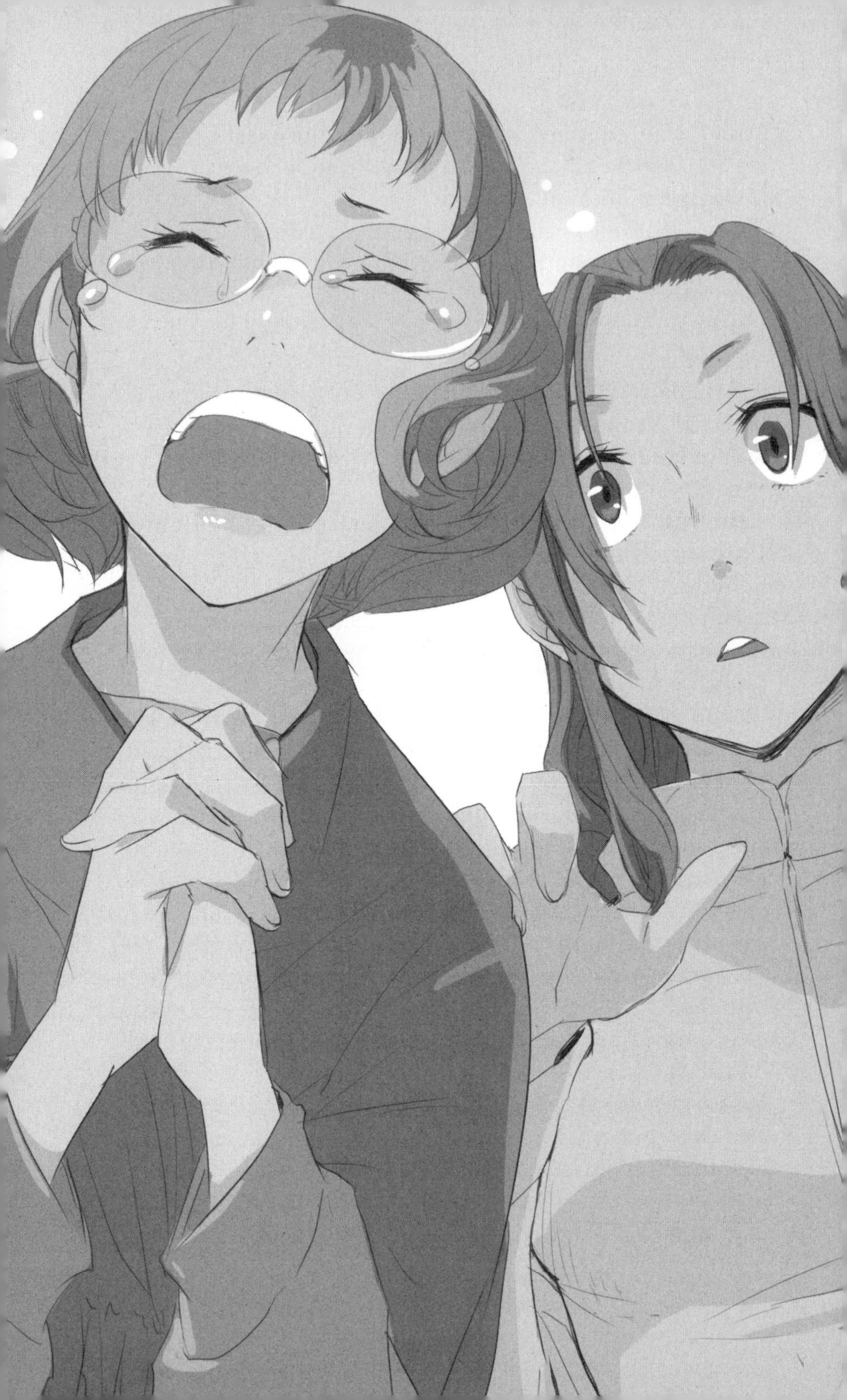

people knew a thing! I'm also the one who made the phone call, s-so, um...if you're going to report someone to the police, please just report me!"

The police*?! You moron!* Biting back the impulse to yell, Pamela stole a glance at Gabriel's face.

The man in black chuckled. "You seem to have the wrong idea, young lady," he said politely.

"Huh...?"

"Over the telephone, we were instructed not to contact the police. In addition...our noble master informed us that the decision of what to do with the criminal was entirely up to us."

"I-in other words...?"

"We may dispose of the culprit as we see fit, here and now."

"Eeeeeeeep?!"

Lana shuddered with terror, and Pamela stepped between them, protecting her. "What do you plan to do with us?"

Gabriel snickered. "It isn't really a question of 'what'... Let's see." He took a wallet from his hip pocket and peered into the coin compartment. "You told us to pay as large a ransom as we could manage, correct?" He'd thought the wallet was empty, but finding a half-dollar coin in a gap, he tossed it to Lana. "This is as much as I can manage at the moment. Any objections?"

Lana, who'd caught the coin, looked dazed for a few moments. Then the situation sank in, and she hastily shook her head. "A-a-a-absolutely not, sir! It's enough—this is enough!"

"In that case, this transaction is settled...but let that be our secret. If word got out that I'd set a price of fifty cents on the young master, my slow and painful death would take years."

It sounded like nothing more than a joke, but the coldness in his eyes indicated he meant every word.

Lana was shaking in her shoes, so Pamela spoke up dubiously in her place. "You mean you're letting us go? Why...?"

"Consider it a demonstration of my respect for the great criminals who made an enemy of the Runorata Family for fifty cents. Besides, I truly am grateful for the support you gave us with that smoke screen. It allowed us to avoid showing the young master needless bloodshed." Gabriel chuckled for a little while, then turned to face the two women and added one quiet remark. "However, should you *press your luck again*... You do understand what will happen, yes?"

He smiled at them with eyes that were colder than ice. Lana and Pamela felt a sharp, frigid *something* race down their spines. Thinking that he probably had every intention of murdering them should something like this happen again, they understood all too clearly that the man meant what he said.

Lana's face had gone dead white, and she seemed ready to topple over. Supporting her, Pamela mustered her courage and briefly replied to this pursuer she'd only just met. "...Thank you. We're in your debt."

"No, we're even."

"Huh?"

Gabriel wasn't looking at them any longer. He was gazing at the boy Juliano had brought, the one who was hurrying toward him. "I haven't seen the young master enjoy himself so much in a very long time. Thus, we're even."

Gabriel walked away toward Cazze, and as if to take his place, Sonia came running. She'd retrieved her guns from the men in military uniforms. When she saw Lana, who was pale-faced and trembling, she cocked her head. "What's the matter? Pamela? Lana? Oh... Did you two fight again? Come ooooon! You shouldn't dooo that."

At the sound of the girl's easygoing rebuke, Pamela pulled on a brave face. "Sorry, sorry. It's fine, Sonia. We aren't fighting." She thumped Lana on the shoulders.

The impact made Lana stagger a little, but she smiled, still teary-eyed and pale. "I'd like to pat myself on the back for not passing out. Come on, tell me I did good."

"Yes, yes. Wow, amazing, you're incredible, Lana."

"Yeah, increeedible!"

Sonia smiled, attempting to join their conversation, but something else caught her attention. She turned in that direction.

"Hey, it's that big bear from earlier."

She looked and sounded so innocent while she pointed. When Lana saw the grizzly that emerged from the smoke screen, her mind finally succumbed to oblivion.

⇔

"Are you all right, young master?" Gabriel called as he approached Cazze.

Cazze looked down. He seemed rather dejected.

"What's the matter?"

"Um... I'm sorry I worried you...," the boy murmured with genuine regret.

Gabriel smiled. "It isn't our job to be angry with you. That task belongs to your family. If we ever scold you, it will be when you've treated their words with contempt."

Juliano picked up where he'd left off, switching out of his usual coarse tone. "However, you should probably prepare for a *very* sound scolding when you return home."

"...Yes." The boy kept his head lowered apologetically.

Gabriel spoke to him quietly. "Did you experience enough to make that scolding worthwhile, young master?"

At that, Cazze's face lit up, and he nodded firmly. "Uh-huh! I'm sure I'll never forget today as long as I live!"

"That's wonderful. Now, let's go home. We'll arrange for a car. Do you have any belongings?"

Since he'd run away from home, Gabriel didn't think he'd have much, but he asked just in case.

Cazze fidgeted a little. "Um, can I ask you for...just one thing?"

"Anything, as long as it's in our power to provide."

"There's somebody I want to take home with me."

"My, my. Bold words." Gabriel hadn't been expecting that request. His eyes widened, and he remembered the boys and girls who'd been nearby. *Is it the young lady with ponytails, or the bespectacled Asian, or one of the three kidnappers? He can't mean one of the boys...*

As various conjectures churned in his mind, the boy pointed at something.

The enormous grizzly that shambled out of the still-expanding smoke screen.

"We made friends earlier! The others say they don't know anything about this bear, and, um, do you think I could keep him at home?"

Far too reckless, far too innocent.

Ordinarily, the giant grizzly could only have been an object of terror, but the boy was treating it like a puppy he'd found.

The twins in black exchanged looks, then smiled back with no hesitation.

"As you wish."

They bowed deferentially to their future master.

⇔

While the bear and the twins confronted each other and the kids were launching their boats into the river, a man was breathing roughly. He was bleeding from the head and sitting in a small boat that had cast off from the shore a little distance away.

"Dammit... I'll kill them... I'll slaughter them all...!" Sarges had managed to escape the twins and the grizzly by a hair.

There was only one emotion left inside him, and in a sense, it might have been fair to call it revenge.

Goose had given him a mission, as a member of the Lemures.

He was no longer able to carry it out.

His mission had been stolen.

As a result, his thirst for revenge was directed at every living creature in sight.

The smoke signal had already gone up.

At this point, he had no way to tell whether Senator Beriam had actually agreed to the deal, but now it would be hopeless either way.

It was possible that this would throw off the operation on the Flying Pussyfoot, too. If that happened, the Lemures' plot wouldn't succeed.

Beneath the paling sky, he began to hear the noise of the approaching train.

It's over. It's all over.

Safe in the escape boat he'd prepared for just such an emergency, Sarges quietly let his malice build.

I'll kill them. It's their fault... This incomprehensible crew—!

He was holding a machine gun. Quietly raising its muzzle, he took aim at the figures on the shore, the boats floating downstream.

Proper form didn't even come into it. He was just braced to shoot.

There was no telling what his accuracy would be like, but he wasn't calm enough to consider things like that at the moment.

Considering the number of bullets he was about to unleash, though, a few people were bound to get lead poisoning.

As if releasing the impulse he'd been forcing down, Sarges began to squeeze the trigger.

But his finger stopped.

Wh-what's that...?

He'd picked up on the same *uneasy feeling* he'd felt earlier.

It was so intense that it halted his impulse in its tracks.

Of the detestable living creatures he saw, most of them had frozen—except for a few who were in boats floating downstream, looking in his direction. Even that enormous grizzly.

What...is it...?

Up...?

It took only about a second.

Sarges's finely honed senses promptly registered what had attracted the attention of the group.

Were they watching the train on the bridge? If so, their expressions were very strange.

The question calmed him down as he turned his attention to the train, too. His Lemures comrades had to have completed their hijacking by now.

Right in the middle of it, he saw a vision in black, red, and pale flesh tones.

The jet-black dress reminded him of a crow.

Skirt fluttering, a black-haired woman with a wounded shoulder leaped lightly off the train and plunged toward the river.

"Cha...Chané?!" Sarges shouted.

According to Goose's plan, they were supposed to find an opportunity during their occupation of the train to get rid of her.

Technically, he should have turned his gun on her and shot her dead.

But he began to move a moment too late.

The woman fell, her long, slim legs shining against a backdrop of the dawn sky and the train.

For just a moment, their beauty and allure made Sarges freeze.

The next moment, a shadow fell over him.

It would have been great if that shadow had been thrown by Chané's dress—

—but the object that appeared above him was a sturdy, extremely heavy wooden crate.

$$\Longleftrightarrow$$

Less than a quarter mile downstream

"Hey, there we go—they're comin' down. So we just have to go get those, huh?

"Man, that's a whole lot earlier than Melody predicted."

"Actually, that train's really bookin', ain't it?"

"Is it, uh… It looks like it's smoking from places besides the smokestack."

"I bet you're seeing things."

The boys in the boats gazed at the crates that were tumbling off the distant train one after another.

"Huh…? Did a black thing just fall off, too?"

"Huh?"

"It looked like someone in a dress…"

"It's my little sister!" "Enough already."

"Hya-haah!"

The earlier commotion was just a distant memory, and the kids had resumed their usual mode of conversation.

A few minutes later, they'd meet a woman who was drifting along, clinging to a crate.

They'd have no idea what sort of fate she would bring them.

"Hey! It's a lady! She really did jump off that train!"

"Whaaaat? …So this sister was cargo, too?!"

"Hey!" "Heeey!" "You okay?!"

"Hya-haah!" "Hya-haaaw."

Or really, whether they'd picked up on it or not—

—the boys would welcome her with smiles, just as they always did.

⇔

Even as he stayed wary of the black-clad men who'd come to stand on either side of him, Cookie gazed at a spot on the train as it passed by.

He was looking at a red human-shaped something that seemed to glide across the sides of the cars.

For a moment, he thought that red *something* had looked his way.

There was no knowing whether Cookie ever realized what it actually was, but as if he were wistfully calling to it, he sent a roar echoing over the early-morning river.

⇔

Meanwhile, the "red something" that had been crawling along the side of the train had noticed the enormous grizzly, too.

At first, he only thought that the young cargo thieves' accomplices were out on the river in boats—but then he saw a huge grizzly standing on the riverbank with its head turned his way.

"…Cookie?"

Inexplicably certain that the grizzly was his former companion, the young man smiled happily. And although he had no reason to be as sure as he was, he was correct.

"Ha-ha!"

Briefly forgetting the situation on the train, he remembered scenes from the past.

No idea what's going on, but wow. Who'd have thought I'd meet up with Cookie again at a time like this…?

Is it even possible for this to be a coincidence?

Thinking of the good old days, just for a moment, the Rail Tracer let Claire Stanfield surface. He gave Cookie a jaunty wave, then nodded firmly.

"I'd expect no less of my world!"

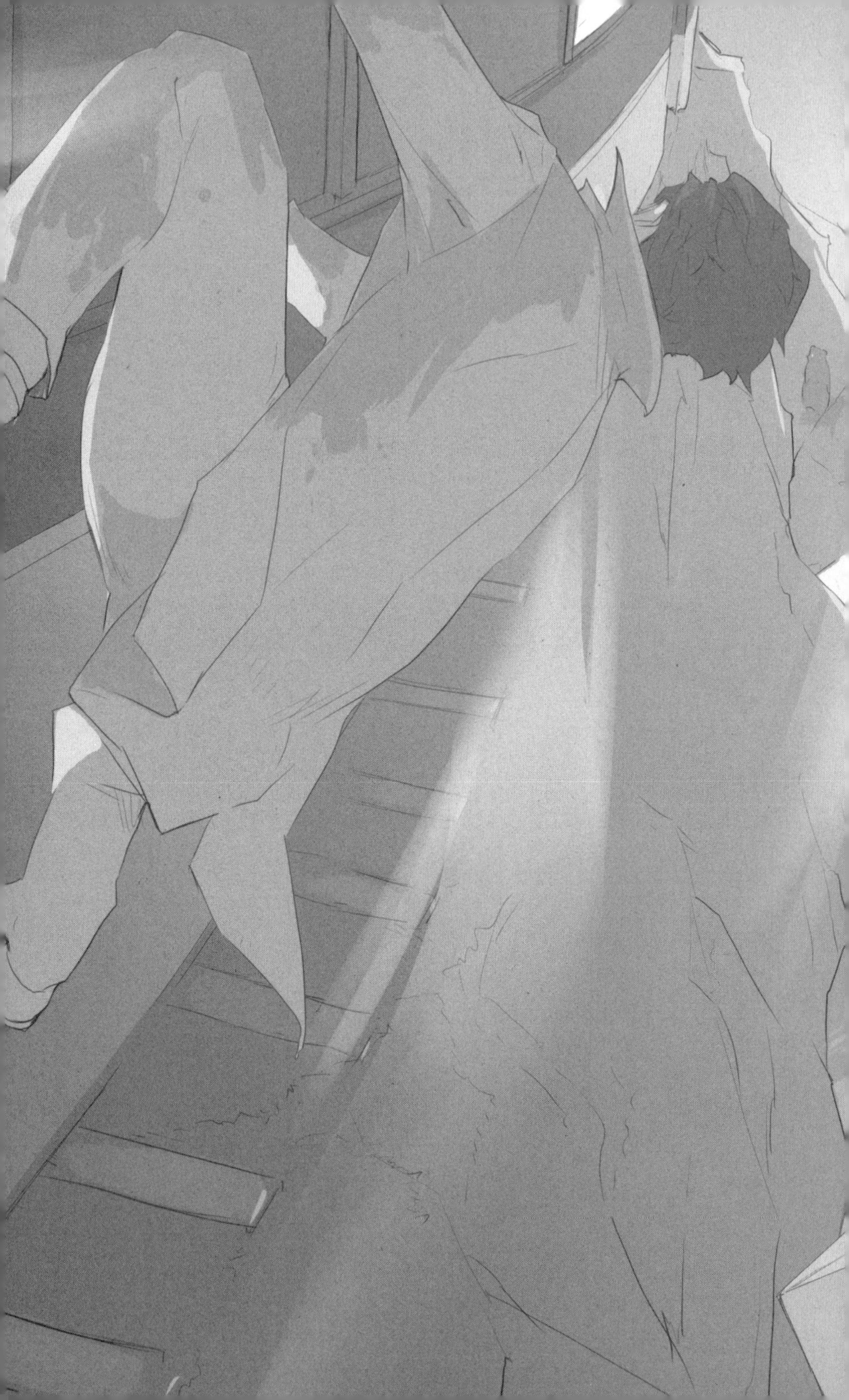

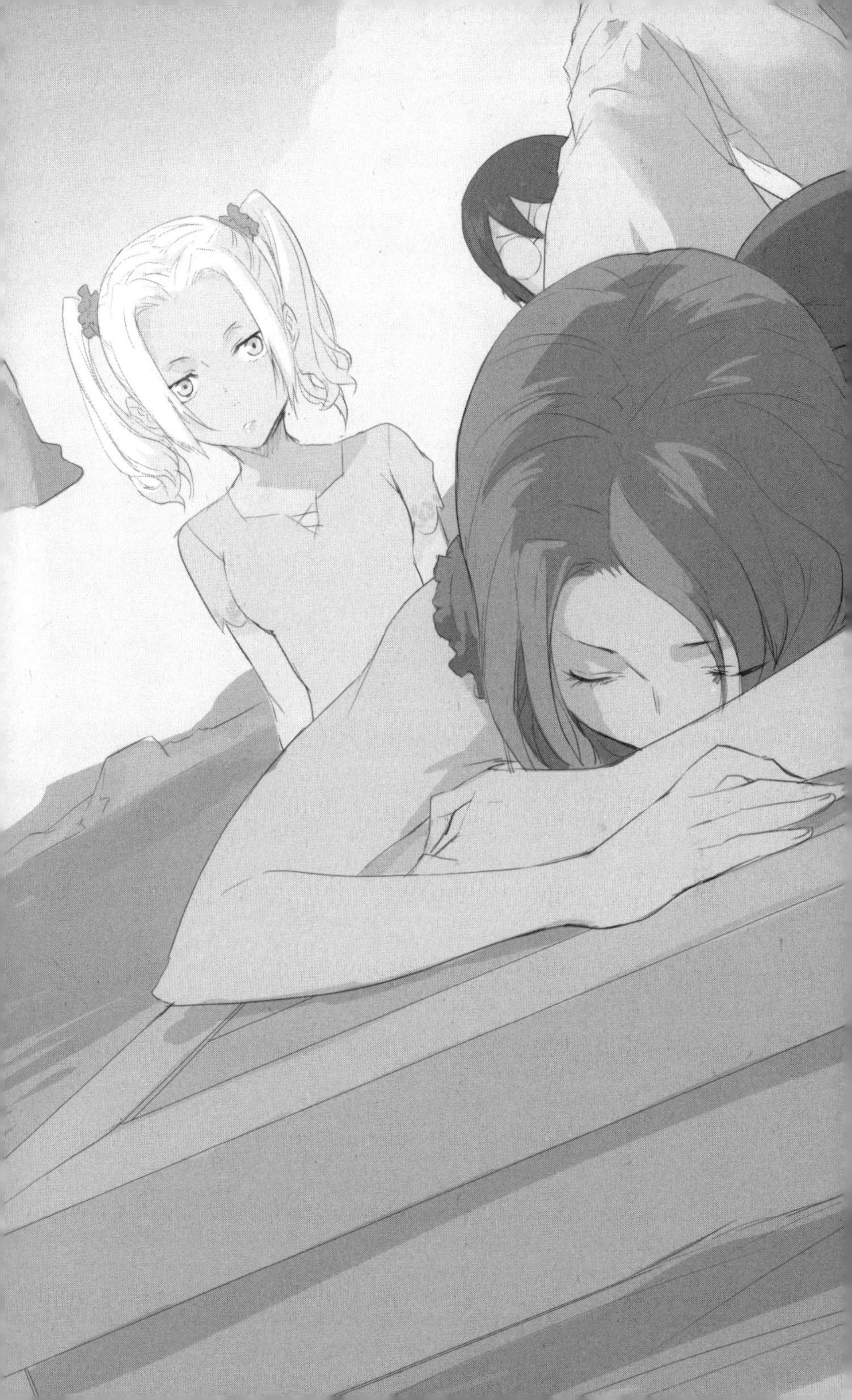

Digression

The Flying Pussyfoot   In a second-class compartment

"Ow, ow, ow, ow! Hngyaah! Ah! WAAaaAAaaAaAah!" Jacuzzi Splot foamed at the mouth, wailing pathetically.

With those screams in his ears, a doctor dressed from head to toe in gray was treating his stomach. "The anesthetic should be working, but…," he murmured.

"Oh… I believe he only thinks it hurts because of how it looks, sir."

"I see. Intriguing."

This was a second-class compartment on the Flying Pussyfoot, a place that had been occupied by terrorists in black suits until just a few moments ago.

Originally, a fearsome group in white suits—unrelated to the ones in black—had been occupying the car, but this man wearing gray was now treating the leader of the colorful delinquents in it.

"Pull yourself together. You're the hero who saved this train, remember?" the doctor in gray told the kid. Practically speaking, this was true. He didn't know exactly how it had happened, but he understood that the boy's group had maneuvered between the black-suited terrorists and the white-suited murderers and liberated the train.

"Waaauuuuh… I-it wasn't anything that impressive…," Jacuzzi said with tears streaming down his face.

Nice, who was watching from beside them, spoke with a wry smile. "Oh, honestly. If you'd only stayed unconscious, maybe we could've had some peace and quiet."

Jacuzzi had been out cold until a few minutes ago, but he'd come to just as they got the worst of his bleeding stopped. Right now, he was wailing while the doctor continued his treatment. It was a pretty sorry sight.

"N-Niiice, that's mean to say."

The gray doctor went on. "You were lucky, though. Even the bullet you took in the stomach doesn't seem to have hit any major organs."

"R-really?!"

"Yes. However, if I'd started treating you three minutes later, it's likely that you would have bled to death."

"Dea…!" This new awareness of the danger he'd been in made Jacuzzi faint again.

Nice heaved a big sigh. "Doctor… Will Jacuzzi…?" She sounded uneasy.

"There's no need to worry. He still wants to live. You can see it in his eyes." As he continued working dexterously, the doctor gave a muffled chuckle from behind the fabric that covered his mouth. "In that case, it is my duty to keep this boy alive. I don't know what he'll do with the rest of his life, but I'll do everything in my power to save him. Even if he's destined to become the worst kind of villain."

"…Jacuzzi is a hero."

"He doesn't seem to think so."

"He is to me… To all of us." Turning a kind smile on Jacuzzi, Nice went on. "More than that, he's our dear friend."

"A friend, hmm…? That's a fine thing. Take good care of him." The words seemed to have some deeper meaning for the gray doctor, and his voice held a variety of emotions. "To hear you speak, it sounds as though many people look up to this fellow."

Like a magician who saw through everything, he made a remark that sounded almost like a prophecy. "You said his name was

Jacuzzi? No doubt he's shouldered the fates of many, and many people will shoulder his destiny." Neatly wrapping a bandage, he went on. "Therefore, any movement he makes will create commensurate waves around him. The connections between humans muddle the fate of the world. They're an oar that's sturdier than anything."

"......?" Nice looked dubious.

"Ah, my apologies. I'm sure I sounded like some conjurer just now, but I wasn't prophesying or telling his fortune. I simply guessed at what would happen."

"......"

"If this boy is pulled into anything, it will affect the lives of many people. He'll be frightened, yes, but I doubt he'll run."

Nice had no response for the magician.

He'd spoken as if he'd seen clear through their lives—and also as if he were pointing out a path to them.

"Live or die, it's up to this boy. Will his ties to you become a shackle that drags him to his death, or a lifeline that pulls him out of death's abyss...? No one knows."

"Please don't say such ominous things... I'll protect Jacuzzi." Firm determination shone in Nice's one remaining eye.

As the gray magician looked at her, the set of his lips softened behind the cloth that hid his face. "I see. That's good to hear. You, Jacuzzi, and your other companions should continue to live for as long as you want to. To the best of your ability, please encourage those around you to live as well."

The magician murmured not to Nice but to some distant, unknown person—or perhaps to himself, a man who'd lost many companions.

"At the very least, I will not let him die here. I promise you that." He nodded.

"The rest of your fate is up to you. I hope you'll become lifelines not just for each other, but for many people."

Epilogue   The White Rabbits Return from the Tea Party

Several hours later   In the truck

In the front seat of the large truck the Runorata Family had sent, Cazze was asleep, breathing peacefully.

After everything had ended, a police van had arrived and arrested the incapacitated military men, one after another. Most of them had been taken straight to a hospital run by the police.

Miraculously, no one had died. However, Sarges was injured so badly that it would take him anywhere from several months to several years to make a full recovery.

Cazze knew nothing about these bloody results, though. He was dreaming, with satisfaction on his face.

He was about to become a bird in a cage again and would spend a while longer wandering through a life as dull as a desert.

The idea didn't torment the boy as much as it had before, though.

Now that he'd learned what it was like outside, his craving could easily have grown more intense, but it hadn't. Dimly, he understood that when he grew up, he'd be able to affect that outside world.

There was an oasis known as "outside," and its water had been sweeter than he'd anticipated. Now that he knew that, he'd have hope on his journey through that boring desert.

*   *   *

This boy, who was far too pure, would later be called an innocent dictator. He would become particularly feared among the gangs of the East, and rumors that he "tamed enormous monsters" in many ways would begin to circulate.

But that's a story for another day.

⇔

In the rattletrap truck

"I swear. I never thought you'd just spill everything at the worst possible time."

"Oh, come on! That's *why* they spared us, so it's fine! Tell me I did good!"

Once everything was over, after saying brief good-byes to Cazze and the delinquents, the three members of Vanishing Bunny made themselves scarce in their old jalopy.

As they rattled down the road that ran parallel to the tracks, Pamela and Lana were entertaining themselves with one of their usual arguments.

"If you'd told him you threw that smoke bomb because you thought it was a real bomb, they would have stuffed us into oil drums and put us on the bottom of the ocean."

"And you're not going to congratulate me on how clever I was to avoid telling him that?!"

"Oh, yes, wow, that was great; your brain's as valuable as a dinosaur fossil. Too bad it wasn't destroyed along with them."

"Now listen, you—!"

"Quit fiiighting."

Sonia had never picked up on how tense the situation had been, and she scolded the other two in her usual laid-back way. "It's all riiight. If we ever end up in real danger, I'm sure Nader will come and save us." She gave an innocent smile.

Rolling her eyes, Lana teased her about the man. "Nader again?

You know, we've been in trouble countless times, but this prince of yours hasn't come to save us once."

"He's not a prince. Nader's a hero, all right? And he promised. I bet we got through those other times because Nader was helping us from the shadows."

Puffing out her cheeks crossly, Sonia recalled the face of her slightly older childhood friend.

If she'd stayed at the scene for just a few more hours, Sonia and her friend would have been reunited. Unfortunately, the chain of coincidences didn't work quite that far in her favor.

After that, when Lana had finally stopped calling her names, Pamela's hands tightened on the steering wheel. "In any case, you told them it was one hundred percent your fault and tried to save me and Sonia, didn't you?"

"Uh, wh-what, are you still scolding me?! You are, aren't you?!"

Lana had done something dangerous without checking with them first, and Pamela really could have screamed at her in a fit. But glancing at her wary face, Pamela just smiled wryly. "Well, uh, you know... Thanks. I did think you were an idiot, but it made me kind of happy."

For a moment, the unexpected honesty made Lana freeze. Then her face turned bright red, and she started flailing her arms, yelling desperately.

"Wha— What are you— Did you just thank me?! C-cut that out! You make it sound like I said those things because I *wanted* you to thank me! I didn't! That was just, uh...spur of the moment!"

"Quit fiiighting."

The mood in the truck was back to normal. Out of nowhere, Pamela thought, *Desert rabbits who keep searching for an oasis, hmm?*

Remembering the metaphor she'd come up with earlier, Pamela looked at Lana's and Sonia's faces and gave a little smile.

These two may actually be my life's biggest oasis.

She didn't say it aloud. She just stepped on the gas.

*　　*　　*

A few minutes later, the women would discover a man with a long sniper's gun lying in the road, and they would be dragged back into the great current.

But that's a story for yet another day as well.

⇔

On the way to New York

Once everything was over, Melody and the others headed straight for New York City.

After they'd retrieved all the bombs, the group split up. Half of them went to meet the individual who had a sales lead, while Melody and the rest started for New York, taking the wounded woman in black with them.

The woman had introduced herself—in writing—as Chané. She seemed to have lost her voice, and she barely responded no matter what they asked her. However, when they mentioned they were going to New York, she'd written *"Please take me with you,"* so there she was, in the back of the truck with them.

Not only had she fallen off the train, but her shoulder was wounded, and she had two large knives. *Suspicious* didn't even begin to cover it, but the delinquents accepted her without giving it much thought.

"Y'know, it feels like a lot happened, but I never did figure out exactly what was going on." Lying down in the back of the truck, the boy with the missing teeth reflected on the events of the past half day. "Like that big ol' bear and the army fellas and the kidnapper dolls—I don't really get how all of that worked out."

"Them's the breaks. If the cops were gonna turn up, we couldn't hang around."

When the men in black had told them that the police were on their way, the boys had hastily retrieved the cargo, then made tracks into the forest.

They hadn't been able to say a proper good-bye to Cazze or his kidnappers, and in the end, they didn't even know what had happened.

"Argh, that's gonna bug me. That's really gonna bug me. I wish I'd gone in the kidnappers' truck. If I had, right about now, we'd be pitching woo."

"...The only thing on your mind is those dolls."

"He's planning to make a pass at my little sisters." "Unforgivable."

"I'll slug you!" "Hya-haah!" "Hya-haw!"

"How did we get from that to this?!"

The conversation had fallen into its familiar pattern, and Melody smiled. Stretching luxuriously, she murmured to the kid with the missing teeth, "Well, it doesn't really matter, does it? Just ask them next time you see them."

"Next time? We don't know their address or nothin'. We don't live anywhere in particular right now, either."

"Even so, I get the feeling we'll see them again. Although I couldn't tell you why...I think they're a lot like us. If we keep living like this, we'll hear each other's names eventually."

"Is that right." The boy looked dubious.

The Asian girl snickered and spoke clearly. "If both our group and their group are travelers wandering the same desert, we'll meet again. You see, no matter how we struggle, there are only so many oases available to us as long as we can't leave the desert... Hya-haah!" "Hya-haw!"

Unusually, Chaini had said something intelligible. Melody giggled, ringing one of her bells softly, and then—

—she gave a remark that was ironic specifically because it came from her.

"It really is what you'd call a matter of time, isn't it?"

After that, they would take up residence in a certain New York mansion and get pulled into all sorts of trouble involving the immortals.

But that's yet another story.

⟺

Their positions were completely different, but all the rabbits continued to wander.

Each of them had found a fleeting oasis in their personal desert.

Either that, or—like the delinquents—their oasis was always with them, in the form of their companions.

Whether or not they wanted to, every one of them eventually stepped into a new desert...

...unaware that those deserts were linked to one another.

They believed that, if they pressed onward, they would at least find a new oasis...

And so their journeys would continue through space and through time.

AFTERWORD

Hello, this is Narita.

Since this volume is a bit of a special case, I'll talk about that first.

Like *1932 Summer*, this book is a revised, expanded version of a bonus from the *Baccano!* anime DVDs.

Just like last time, I imagine some people are thinking, *After I spent all that money to collect the DVDs!* If this is you, I'm really sorry.

As I wrote in the afterword for *1932 Summer*, my personal opinion is that turning short stories that ran in *Dengeki Bunko MAGAZINE* or novels I wrote as DVD bonuses into regular books is the same thing as when a movie is shown in theaters, sold as DVDs and Blu-rays, and then broadcast uncut on TV. Either that, or these are different, "director's cut" versions.

Why am I releasing this one as a regular book now? Those of you who are in the middle of the *1935* arc probably know already, but a certain character who appeared in this volume is scheduled to turn up as a major character in *1935-C*, the third volume in that series. I thought it would be more natural to release this story as a book, rather than rearrange the content and rewrite it.

That said, it's already been five years since I wrote this story. When I went back and read it, quite a bit of it was embarrassing; however, except for adding the "Digression" sections, I used almost all of it just as it was.

There's a strong comedic tone to this one, and it's a bit different from the usual *Baccano!* books. Still, I hope you'll see that this world does have an easygoing side and have fun with it.

I also hope you'll look forward to the continuation of the *1935* arc, in which the characters you encountered in this laid-back setting will be dropped into a much harsher one.

That's probably enough explanation and advertising, so I'll segue to talking about what I've been up to recently.

I ate like a pig and drank like a fish over New Year's and have been paying for it in the form of aggravated gastritis and reflux esophagitis, but I'm on the mend. However, I've got one of those awkward personalities that goes, *Am I healed up yet? Okay, let's find out: I'll pig out today, and if nothing happens, I'm fully healed!* So I pig out, and as a result, I end up with gastritis and reflux esophagitis from eating and drinking too much. I'm starting to think it's less that I'm "awkward" and more that I'm dumb, but, well, facing that reality won't fill me up.

When I told a friend, "It's so weird. When I was in school, I could eat almost twice this much and still be fine," the friend said, "You hole up at home and do nothing but write books, you're past thirty, and you're totally out of shape. What made you think you could eat the same amount of food as you did when you had a two-hour commute to school, one way?"

Aging.

That phrase, *past thirty*, keeps echoing in my head.

Come to think of it, the debut work that came out right as I was graduating from college was *Baccano!* It's already been a decade since then. It's only natural that I don't heal as quickly anymore and that I get out of breath from climbing the stairs...I mean, setting aside the view that I just don't get enough exercise.

That reminds me...

My tenth anniversary.

Yes, a month before this book came out, on February 10, I celebrated a full ten years as a professional writer!

Back when I debuted, I worried whether I'd still be able to keep myself properly fed by working as a writer ten years down the road. Now those days are a fond memory... And here I am, ten years later— Wait! Thanks to that reflux esophagitis, I guess I'm not eating properly!

I didn't anticipate that my own aging—or rather, my lifestyle habits—would defeat my dream, but luckily, I'm still making a living as a writer.

This is all thanks to the members of the editorial department, and to everyone who buys my books!

Really, thank you so much!

At the point in time when I'm writing this afterword, nothing's been officially announced, but I'm writing various new books for Dengeki Bunko and other companies. The continuations of *1935*, *DRRR!!*, and my other series are on the schedule as well, of course, so please give me your continued support!

I'll keep doing my best so that I'll be able to work as a writer for another twenty or thirty years.

I hope you'll be patient and stick with me!

*The regular thank-yous start here.

To my supervising editor, Wada (Papio), the rest of the Dengeki Bunko editorial department, and the copy editors. To the designers, who make my books look sharp. To everyone in the publicity, production management, and marketing departments.

To the people who are constantly taking care of me: my family and friends, and other writers and illustrators.

To the staff of the *Baccano!* anime, who gave me the opportunity to create this novel.

To Katsumi Enami, who gave a bonus novel written five years ago a new soul with these splendid illustrations.

And to everyone who read this book.

All the people mentioned above have my deepest gratitude. Thank you very much!

Please look out for me through the next ten years as well!

January 2013, Ryohgo Narita